Kit and Drew Coons

Challenge *in the* Evergreen State

A Dave and Katie Adventure

Challenge *in the* Evergreen State

ISBN: 979-8-89686-246-8

Library of Congress Control Number: 2024927572

Illustrations by Julie Sullivan (MerakiLifeDesigns.com)

First Edition

 Printed in the United States

24 23 22 21

20   1 2 3 4 5

Challenge
in the
Evergreen State

A Dave and Katie Adventure

Kit and Drew Coons

Novels in the *Challenge Series*

Challenge for Two

Challenge Down Under

Challenge in Mobile

Jeremy's Challenge

Challenge in the Golden State

Challenge in the Evergreen State

"Novels in the Challenge Series took place in different, interesting locations. The authors really captured the culture and feel of all these areas and transported me along on the adventures." Amazon reader

"My favorite novels ever." Retired Reader

"I just finished novel five in the Challenge Series. The characters are believable, the story lines are engaging and the adventures are exciting!" Retail Customer

"I'm not one who normally sits still but really enjoyed this fun, light-hearted, interesting series." Retail Customer

"I am in love with the Challenge Series. My mom, sister and I read them all together." Teenage Reader

"Absolutely love these stories! Good wholesome, family adventures!" Amazon Reader

Acknowledgments

This novel would not be possible without professional editing and proofreading by Jayna Richardson. The artwork and cover were created by Julie Sullivan. We also thank our reviewers Leslie Mercer, Marlys Johnson, and Eunice Schmidt, who read the early manuscript and made valuable suggestions.

Special thanks to Captain Eric Anderson of Washington Department of Fish and Wildlife, called DFW, who met with us and gave the most valuable insights into the crimes of poaching and wild animal trafficking. All the DFW officers we have met are courteous, helpful, and dedicated to the sustainability of Washington's rich resources of fish and wildlife for everyone.

Everybody needs beauty as well as bread, places to play in and pray in, where nature may heal and give strength to body and soul.

John Muir

Principal Characters

Primary Characters from Previous Novels

Dave and Katie Parker • Semi-retired couple in their mid-sixties from Mobile, Alabama. Dave is a forensic accountant. Katie is a former science teacher.

Jeremy and Denyse Parker • Dave and Katie's son and accounting firm junior partner and his Australian wife. Their children are Katelyn (7) and David (3).

Sandra Travnikov • Denyse's twenty-one-year-old sister-in-law. A war refugee to Australia from Ukraine.

Jeff and Tara Moynihan • Conservation advocates and owners of an outdoors-oriented sporting goods store in Northern California.

New Primary Characters

Bethany Turner • Prosecuting attorney in Seattle's DA's office; Casey's girlfriend.

Casey Carpenter • Poorly paid director of Washington Coalition for Sustainability, a struggling nonprofit; Bethany's boyfriend.

Anton Stegall • Manager of an investment portfolio.

Aaron Wierzbowski • Washington Department of Fish and Wildlife (DFW) detective.

Willis Boone • Pioneer Spirit Militia member.

Brian Manning nicknamed "Buddy" • Willis's helper.

Andrew Jackson • Captain of the Pioneer Spirit Militia.

Wilma Stansky • Jackson's wife.

British Columbia
N
W E
S
Vancouver City
Vancouver Island
Strait of Juan de Fuca
Victoria
Salish Sea
Port Townsend
Port Angeles
Forks
Deer Park
Sequim
La Push
Hood Canal
Puget Sound
Poulsbo
Winslow
Seattle
Bremerton
SeaTac Airport
Olympic Mountains
Shelton
Tacoma
Gig Harbor
Gray's Harbor
Olympia
Pacific Ocean
Washington State
Mt. Rainier

Prologue

Two emaciated black bear cubs huddled together in the corner of a wire cage. They cowered and hid their eyes when shadows loomed over them. The acrid odor of tobacco smoke awoke their instinctive fear and desire to escape.

"These are what I've currently got. One's male, the other female," a man with a gruff voice announced.

"Where'd you get 'em?" asked his potential customer.

"A tourist took their mother home as a rug. We pulled these two out of a tree in the mountains using a telescoping pole with a neck loop."

"I need a live exhibit for an exclusive club. How much?"

"Five thousand dollars for either bear. Or I could let you have both for eight thousand."

The buyer responded, "I only need one. My view tank isn't big enough for two bears. They look sick, though. If it dies, I'd want my money back."

"They took some time to get onto cow milk. You might give your best customers an experience bottle feeding them. They can really suck when they've gone a day without food. Which one do you want?"

"I'll take the male. Customers will perceive a male as having more fearsome potential. How long will he stay small?"

"About eighteen months, depending on how much you feed him." The man opened the cage door, reached in, pulled the little male out, and forced him into a cat carrier. He snickered. "When he gets too big, you can sell him as a rug. I'll buy back his gallbladder to resell."

Once separated, both cubs started squalling. "Don't worry. He'll get used to being alone," said the seller. "Let me show you what else I've got."

Chapter One

Katie Parker enjoyed the combined odors of flowers, baked goods, and fresh fish filling Seattle's Pike Place Market. The hustle-bustle of the market fascinated her son, Jeremy, Aussie daughter-in-law, Denyse, and grandchildren. *What an attractive couple Jeremy and Denyse make*, she thought. *Denyse is a wonderful mother and wife to Jeremy.* She felt a pang of regret at the memory of doubting their marriage at first. Overwhelming love and gratitude pushed all other feelings away.

"Did you see that man throw the big fish and the other man catch it?" Denyse asked her seven-year-old daughter, Katelyn.

"Why doesn't Daddy throw the fish he and Grandpa catch?"

"That's because fish are slippery," Jeremy answered while pushing three-year-old David in a stroller. "We would probably drop them."

"We'll see if that's true the next time we go fishing in Alabama, sweetheart," answered Denyse.

Bright and shiny things for sale and the throngs of excited people mesmerized the children and Denyse as well. "This is a part of America I haven't seen before," she said.

A small cheese factory and shop captivated Jeremy. Katie darted into a French bakery to buy treats for all. Denyse bought coffee for herself and Jeremy at the original Starbucks. The family shared the baked goods on a wide patio facing west overlooking Seattle's harbor and Puget Sound. In the distance, the snow-covered Olympic Mountains dominated the horizon between evergreen forests and a bright blue sky. Temperatures on the late June day hovered at sixty-five degrees in low-humidity air.

"What a beautiful day!" exclaimed Denyse.

"I expected Washington to be rainy," commented Jeremy. "I'll bet Mobile is hot and humid right now."

Katie tapped a couple of times on her cell phone. "Ninety-four degrees with ninety-six percent humidity."

Jeremy looked at Denyse. "Want to move to Washington, sweetheart?"

"Hold on, you two. Seattle is rainy about eight months a year—"

"Look at that!" Jeremy interrupted his mother and pointed to the south where a massive snow-covered mountain loomed.

Katie tapped some more. "That's 14,410-foot Mount Rainier. Over two hundred feet of snow fall there each year. The mountain is considered an active volcano."

"Active?" Denyse's tone indicated concern for her children.

"But Rainier hasn't erupted for over five hundred years," Katie added.

"So the volcano is sleeping?" Katelyn asked.

"I guess so. Only with a heart of fire." Katie pointed to Seattle's waterfront visible below. "There's the aquarium. They have all sorts of fish, seals, and even sea otters. I've made reservations for tomorrow."

"Will Dad be able to join us?" asked Jeremy.

"Maybe for supper."

* * *

"Mr. Parker, the prosecution has shown the men and women of this jury that you are a certified forensic accountant. We have entered your thorough report to the city of Seattle as exhibit number one. Over the last two days, you have read detailed sections of that report for the record and explained them in a professional manner."

Dave Parker watched the assistant district attorney trying the case. Bethany Turner was a somewhat plain, dour-faced woman in her mid-thirties in makeup that made her look harsher and older. She wore a dark blue business suit. *Did she even try a comb or brush this morning?* he asked himself while looking at her mussed shoulder-length dark hair.

"Now, in layman's terms, would you mind summarizing your findings for our jury?" The prosecutor then used her full arm in a broad gesture to indicate twelve bored-looking jurors. "They have patiently endured your many technical details."

Dave suppressed a smile at her attempt to endear herself to the jury by recognizing their patience. He cleared his throat before speaking. "The defendant, Mr. Anton Stegall, offered to manage customized investment portfolios under the general title of 'Your Golden Parachute.' But Mr. Stegall actually purchased very few stocks. Rather, he created fictional portfolios in retrospect with stocks based on the records of actual market performances. Mr. Stegall could thereby pump up the apparent returns of beginning clients, enticing them to invest more. He created extravagant payouts for celebrities and notable public figures, then asked for their testimonials. But when an obscure investor wanted to withdraw funds, for which Mr. Stegall required a thirty-day notice, the accused loaded their fictional portfolio with purchases of actual losers, which minimized the payout.

"Prior to his arrest, Mr. Stegall had transferred large amounts to offshore accounts and used the remainder to support his lavish lifestyle, including a condo in Las Vegas. The defendant maintained a high and glamorous public profile, which attracted even more investors. He ultimately defrauded thousands of individuals, including senior citizens who had invested their life savings, several 501c charitable organizations, and company pension plans. The entire operation was a cleverly disguised Ponzi scheme." Dave noticed that several jurors had leaned forward to catch this concise summary after days of obscure accounting details, haggling between the lawyers, and delays. He saw the defendant glaring at him with undisguised loathing.

The assistant DA stroked her chin and nodded as if she understood for the first time herself. "That makes sense, considering the proof supplied in your report." She paused. "One last question, Mr. Parker. Do you believe beyond any reasonable doubt that Anton Stegall is guilty of fraud according to the standards of accounting?"

Dave inwardly laughed at the prosecutor's theatrical demeanor, which she had practiced during rehearsals with him. "I have no doubt that Anton Stegall is guilty of fraud." Several jurors unconsciously nodded.

Ms. Turner turned and approached the jury. "There you have it, ladies and gentlemen. Authoritative testimony by a renowned expert." She nodded at the judge. "No other questions, Your Honor. The prosecution rests."

Judge Harmon stirred and asked, "Counsel for the defense, are you ready to cross examine?"

"Yes, I am, Your Honor." The defendant's attorney bounced to his feet, apparently eager to set things straight. He took a position before Dave. "Mr. Parker, you own an accounting firm named Parker and Associates. Is that correct?"

"Yes. I own the firm with two junior partners."

"Several years ago, your firm experienced financial difficulty due to sloppy work. Isn't that correct?"

Dave noticed the jurors perking up. He thought, *Because all the evidence shows guilt, the defense's only chance is to discredit me.* He answered, "No."

"But financial disclosures show loss of most clients and almost no revenue for several years."

"That was Bayshore Accounting. I bought the firm from the former owners. Since then, there has been no sloppy work." Dave noticed the jury, less bored, following the exchange.

His accusation planted to create doubt, the defense attorney shrugged to communicate disbelief to the jury. "So you say, Mr. Parker." He stared at Dave. "In your so-called 'thorough report' you acknowledged that you had not been able to trace all the investment funds. About three million dollars is unaccounted for."

"That is correct."

"Doesn't that constitute sloppy work on your part?"

"No. This means Mr. Stegall spent or hid the funds well. And his condo in Las Vegas could imply undocumented gambling losses." Dave heard the jury twitter with interest.

The attorney turned to the bench. "Objection! Your Honor, the witness speculates about gambling without admitted evidence."

Judge Harmon sighed. "Sustained. The jury will disregard Mr. Parker's last statement about gambling losses."

The defense attorney nodded his head and smirked with self-satisfaction before resuming his questions. "You said that you believed my client to be guilty. Since you are paid by the prosecution, you're more or less obligated to say that. Isn't that correct?"

"No."

"But shouldn't you wait for a decision by a jury, before pronouncing a man guilty?"

"The city's representative asked what I believe. I answered truthfully. The records clearly indicate fraud. Hire your own accountant to check that. Oh, wait. You did. He called asking me to explain the report I had provided to the city of Seattle." Dave heard the jury snicker.

The attorney ignored his own blunder. "Mr. Parker, I understand that you're an amateur sleuth. Amateurs often see crimes where there are none. Isn't that correct?"

"Objection!" shouted the prosecutor. "Counsel for the defense is badgering the witness."

"Overruled," Judge Harmon returned. "Mr. Parker seems to be doing just fine." Audible chuckles came from the jury box. The judge turned to Dave. "You may answer the question, Mr. Parker."

"In the process of investigations with my wife, I've been threatened, shot at twice, punched in the face, knocked down, and poisoned. In our last experience, we were framed for homicide and drug dealing then thrown into jail. In every instance, we've persisted to uncover actual crimes. Convictions of criminals followed each discovery." Dave heard jury members laughing in admiration of his response. A few jurors gave disgusted looks at the defense attorney. The judge grinned.

Flustered, the defense attorney continued, "You are from Mobile, Alabama, correct?"

"Yes."

"And yet the city of Seattle hired you when plenty of qualified local accountants are available?"

"Maybe we Alabamians charge less."

More laughter came from the jury box. The judge silenced the jurors with a stern look.

"I have a different theory, Mr. Parker. The DA's office hired you because you've always been a strong supporter of the police. Hasn't that biased you against my client?"

"Would you rather I be a strong supporter of the criminals?" The courtroom roared with spontaneous laughter at Dave's quip and subtle implication of the defense attorney.

"Your Honor, the witness implies that my client is a criminal. I insist that statement be stricken from the court record."

Judge Harmon suppressed his own laughter and ruled, "Agreed. The jury is instructed to disregard Mr. Parker's last words." He paused and looked at the defense counsel. "Is the defense about finished with this witness?"

Stegall's lawyer sighed. "No further questions, Your Honor."

"You may step down, Mr. Parker."

As Dave left the courtroom, he saw a woman, presumably the defendant's sister or girlfriend, glowering with hatred at him.

Chapter Two

"We're all having a wonderful time here in Washington," said Katie as she and Dave lingered over hot tea after supper in their high-rise hotel's restaurant. "You're a genius for inviting us to accompany you at this trial. The luxury suite furnished by the city is big enough for our whole family."

Dave smiled. "Well, I'd be just rattling around and bored by myself in that suite. Do you think Jeremy and Denyse will get Katelyn and David to sleep?"

"Sure. The kids are worn out from touring the city and Woodland Park Zoo. Chihuly Garden and Glass didn't interest them. What they liked best was riding the monorail and streetcar public transports." After a moment of silence Katie added, "I was getting bored in Alabama. I take care of our grandkids, go fishing with you, keep up the house while you're working, and sit in hotel rooms while you're at a trial. I really needed a diversion."

"Well, I'm glad you came. All of you being here makes this fun for me too."

Katie tried to communicate her feelings more clearly. "Actually, I may need more than a diversion. Rather something challenging and significant to do." She paused while Dave waited. "Babysitting, fishing, and following you around is playing in the shallow end of the pool for me. You're involved in serious legal cases serving justice. Jeremy is building up the firm while you concentrate on forensic cases. You know that our son is developing quite a reputation in south Alabama. Everybody, regardless of religion or political persuasion, appreciates his well-known 'Do for others what you would have them do for you,' policy. He's been approached by both political parties to run for the state senate next fall."

Dave shook his head. "I did *not* know that. But I *am* getting older. Not hearing and forgetting are in close contest when I'm concentrating on a case."

Katie rolled her eyes. "Don't I know it. Maybe you've got so much in your head that you have to forget something to make room for anything new."

Dave laughed. "Maybe so. But getting back to Jeremy, he acts goofy sometimes, especially when trying to lighten a tense moment. But when the situation requires it, our son is the most practical and deepest thinker of any of us. He also has the ability to lead people into working together. They recognize his unselfishness."

"And how about Denyse?" asked Katie.

"What about Denyse?"

"Denyse is so very talented and capable. She needs nothing from me other than occasional childcare. Mobile's Board of Education has asked her to help upgrade mathematics programs all over the city."

Dave nodded. "She reminds me of you when you were her age. You ran programs to interest kids in science all over south Alabama. Later you organized dozens of marriage enrichment programs. You've been as tough as a hickory nut solving some big mysteries with me. I'm hearing you say that now you feel dead in the water."

"Correct! I feel like I'm just a babysitter and a husband follower."

"Maybe something will turn up. Knowing you, you'll go all in."

"Yes, I will." Feeling better after sharing, Katie changed the topic. "How did the trial go today?"

"The jury has started deliberation. We might get a verdict soon."

"What's the prospect for a guilty verdict?"

Dave first recounted the cross examination, at which Katie chuckled. Then he shook his head. "The defense produced local character witnesses, cited community involvement, and documented financial contributions to local nonprofits by the defendant. Juries are hard to convince with details of accounting against public persona. And Seattle's prosecutor comes across as a human barracuda."

"Who wouldn't believe you, though? You ooze integrity and competence. The jury, especially the women, would have noticed your dignity and patrician good looks."

"So we should have put you on the stand for the men?" Dave shook his head. "Trials are supposed to be about the defendant and evidence, not the witnesses."

"In a perfect world." Katie shrugged and changed the subject. "Tomorrow, we're going to explore Seattle's waterfront and visit the aquarium. We hope to have supper at a seafood restaurant called Ivar's. Think you could join us on the waterfront at about six?"

"Both the courthouse and our hotel are close by. I should be able to."

* * *

As they walked toward the aquarium, Jeremy expressed regret. "I'm sorry Dad is missing this. He never gets tired of looking at fish."

"Don't worry about your father," returned Katie. "Dave has a strong sense of justice. He hates the waiting at trials. But this crime was so egregious that he'll get tremendous satisfaction if they get a conviction."

Dad's not the only one with a strong sense of justice, thought Jeremy. *Mom's clever when she sniffs the smoke of a mystery and tenacious in finding the fire.* He looked at his short and thin mother, now in her later sixties and having survived two bouts of cancer. He appreciated her no-nonsense approach to life yet compassionate nature. *She's a perfect counterpart to Dad's curiosity and thoroughness.*

Jeremy glanced at his Australian wife, who stood nearly a head taller than his mother. *They say a man frequently marries someone like his mother. Denyse is a lot like Mom, only with a double helping of compassion. They are both teachers. Both good mothers too.*

Inside the aquarium, brightly colored fish captured even young David's attention. He could hardly take his eyes away from the tanks of jellyfish slowly undulating under lights that highlighted their translucent bodies. But antics by the seals and sea otters appealed more to Katelyn.

* * *

Dave sat reading about the historic Oregon Trail in the waiting area of Seattle's Municipal Court while remaining available to clarify testimony, if recalled. He marveled at the fortitude of the 1840s pioneers. He knew Katie regarded that history from the viewpoint of wives reluctant to leave their extended families and livelihood for a dubious future. *Maybe Katie will agree to rent a car and drive home along the historic sites,* Dave hoped.

"Mr. Parker?"

Dave looked up to see a blue-eyed young man in his thirties who looked like a handsome actor depicting an unshaven woodsman. Except, rather than buckskin, he wore jeans, a pullover knit shirt, and well-used hiking boots with a worn knapsack over one shoulder. Dave had noticed him among the spectators in the courtroom when he testified. "I can't talk about the trial."

"Of course. I need to ask you about something important, please."

The court bailiff's voice shouted down the hall. "The jury is returning with a verdict."

Dave saw people hurrying back into the courtroom. "I'm allowed back in the courtroom now. If you don't mind, I'd like to hear this."

"Me too," answered the young man.

The courtroom seats had filled quickly. Dave and the young man stood with several others along the back wall. The normal courtroom procedure ensued, culminating with Judge Harmon asking the jury foreman, "Would you read your verdict?"

Despite the preponderance of evidence, Dave found himself holding his breath.

"We the jury find the defendant guilty of all charges."

Expressions of joy erupted in the courtroom. The jurors looked gratified. The young man next to Dave raised both arms in exultation and said, "Hallelujah!"

The judge reclaimed order and then remanded Anton Stegall into custody. As he thanked the jury and scheduled victim impact statements to begin the following week, Dave slipped out the back, followed by the young man.

In the hallway, Dave stopped and asked, "Now what can I do for you, Mister . . ."

The young man fumbled for words. "Casey. I mean Carpenter. My name is Casey Carpenter. Please call me Casey."

"Okay, Casey. Why do you wish to talk to me?"

"Tara Moynihan said that you could help us."

"Tara? You mean the Tara Moynihan who lives in Redwood Hills, California?"

"Yes, sir."

"How do you know Tara?"

"She and her husband Jeff are involved in the same causes as we are. I mean as me and my girlfriend."

Dave looked at his watch. *5:11*. He knew that Katie and the others would be expecting him at Ivar's at six. Yet he thought, *If Casey is an associate of Tara and Jeff's, then you need to be hospitable. Remember how Tara saved you and Katie.*

"How about this, Casey? I'm meeting my family at Ivar's Fish Bar at six. Would you like to join us for dinner as my guest? We could hear about your cause and catch up on Tara's activities."

The young man grinned. "Sure. Can I bring my girlfriend? She knows Tara too. But we might be a few minutes late."

"Of course. We'll look for you at six or a little after."

Chapter Three

Dave rushed to the hotel to change out of his business suit. Wearing walking shoes and casual clothes, he hurried to the waterfront. He found his family seated on an outside deck over the water outside Ivar's. Raucous seagulls surrounded them. Katelyn tossed French fries to the birds, resulting in free-for-all squabbles and loud squawking. Her parents urged Katelyn on while Katie watched David asleep in the stroller.

A blatantly false sign nearby made Dave laugh because of its absurdity.

DO NOT BE AFRAID OF OVERFEEDING
SEAGULLS ARE DAINTY EATERS

Jeremy smiled when he saw his father. "How'd it go, Dad?"

"Guilty on all charges."

Jeremy stood to give his father a high five. Denyse gave him a hug. And Katie simply said, "I'm proud of you, Dave."

Dave nodded solemnly to her. "Your opinion matters more to me than everybody else's in the world," he finally said.

"Well, now we can order," suggested Jeremy.

"Could we wait just a few minutes?" Dave asked. "I invited some friends of Tara and Jeff's to join us."

Twenty minutes later Casey appeared with a familiar young woman carrying an attaché case. Dave had to look twice. He recognized Bethany Turner, but she looked completely different without makeup, her hair in a cute ponytail, and dressed casually. *Without that business suit, she is thin and athletic-looking,* Dave internally acknowledged.

"Congratulations on your verdict, Ms. Turner."

Bethany smiled. "Thanks to you, Mr. Parker! I couldn't have gotten that conviction without your thorough study of sketchy bookkeeping and your credibility on the witness stand. Let's use first names now, okay?"

"Of course, Bethany." Having worked with her professionally, Dave felt unnerved by Bethany's personality shift. He marveled at Bethany's transformation as she recounted Dave's clever cross-examination answers and mimicked the voices for his family.

"Records and paper-trail evidence hardly mattered," Bethany concluded. "The jurors simply believed Dave."

Dave introduced his family. Casey asked Katelyn and David simple questions and made them laugh. Bethany immediately related to Jeremy and Denyse. "I've learned a lot about you two," she said.

"How would you know anything about us?" wondered Denyse.

"As a prosecutor, I had to research our primary witness. I called some previous clients and associates. People in Mobile." Bethany pointed at Dave. "You've helped him and Katie in some serious matters. And of course, Tara told us about each of you too."

A middle-aged and heavily tattooed waitress appeared. "What would you like to drink?"

Dave spoke first. "I'll take iced tea with lemon." The other Parkers ordered tea or various soft drinks. "You can order beer, if you prefer," he said to Casey and Bethany. Which they did.

After the drinks arrived, the group ordered a variety of dishes: clam and smoked salmon chowders, traditional fish and chips with Alaskan cod or halibut. "What is halibut?" asked Denyse.

"It's like a giant flounder but fileted to avoid bones," answered Dave.

"Oooh, I like flounder. I'll have that," she returned.

"I'm looking at the three-piece Cajun-n-chips," said Jeremy. "I wonder if it's like our Cajun cooking in Mobile."

"Only one way to find out," suggested Katie.

Jeremy looked at the waitress. "Okay, I'll try Cajun-n-chips."

After everybody had ordered, Denyse asked Bethany, "What did Tara tell you about us?"

"She said that all you Parkers are honorable people and as clever as hell." After that remark, Bethany looked pointedly at Casey.

"Let me explain," Casey began. "I run a conservation nonprofit, Washington Coalition for Sustainability." He passed out simple business cards. "Tara is developing a West-Coast reputation for activism to preserve wild places, and she follows my blog. She contacted me to ask about areas where a second Outdoors Always store might thrive. That's the name of her outdoors recreation store in California. I suggested Olympia, which is roughly midway between Mt. Rainer, Olympic National Park, and Washington's coastline. She needed a large space, maybe a former department store or car dealership. Bethany and I scouted some possible sites beforehand and then guided Tara when she came up here last winter. Tara asked Bethany what sort of work she did." Casey looked at Dave and Katie. "After hearing Bethany's profession, Tara told a fantastic story about you solving a crime in California."

"Tara has a deep-rooted suspicion of law enforcement officers," Dave commented.

Bethany nodded. "I picked up on that from some comments she made about deputies raiding her commune in Wisconsin. Afterwards I downplayed my role as an officer of the court. Tara is a hoot. We had so much fun together. She's both wily and bold. She told us plenty. Did a bad cop really try to shoot you?"

Katie answered, "Yes. Tara drew the cop's attention to herself while we escaped. Tara also saved Dave after the same cop had poisoned him with fentanyl. She even went undercover to help us break up an opioid ring. Dave and I think of Tara like a second daughter after Denyse."

Denyse spoke up, "Tara was Jeremy's first love."

Bethany leaned forward. "So it's true that Tara tried to steal Jeremy away when he was a teenager? They hardly seem compatible!"

Jeremy laughed. "Yes, I once had a crush on Tara. Any eighteen-year-old would have. She was a twenty-two-year-old free spirit." He looked at his wife. "But my only true love is Denyse."

Denyse patted Jeremy's hand. "I know that's true."

Jeremy nodded. "Tara was a bit of a con artist back then and could have succeeded in getting my college fund. But she did the right thing by not deceiving me."

"And Jeremy made a good choice himself," Denyse added.

Bethany looked at Denyse and her children then nodded. "Boy, did he ever. I wish I had made better choices."

During that sincere moment, Katie noticed Casey glancing at Bethany. "Tara later made a good choice herself by marrying Jeff."

Their food arrived. After sorting out who ordered what, the Parkers bowed their heads for a brief prayer, to which Casey first then Bethany complied.

Dave spoke first as they started to eat. "So Casey, why did Tara suggest you contact us?"

"She suspects something nefarious is happening in Washington. Her network of fellow outdoors advocates have reported the sparsity of wildlife and a general mood of concern. That made Bethany and me reexamine comments being made on my website. A lot of people who follow my website think Washington's natural resources are being abused."

"Environmentalists always think that."

Casey smiled. "Yes, they do. And frequently they're right. But our group is about conservation and sustainability. We have outdoors people of all types—some environmentalists, hikers and campers, hunters, fishermen, road bicyclists, wild animal lovers, mountain bikers, lumberjacks, nature lovers of all kinds—"

Bethany interrupted him, "In the DA's office, I started noticing complaints about possible abuses we don't have the resources to follow up on. Citizens sense the decline of wild ecosystems." Her grim professional persona had returned. Then she sounded almost plaintive. "I can't discern any pattern but have a bad feeling about things."

"Do you think some public officials could be complicit?" asked Katie.

"If so, probably not many. Washington's Department of Fish and Wildlife or DFW officers are nearly all sportsmen or hikers, and many consider themselves environmentalists. Same with the US Forest Service, National Park rangers, and state park employees. Police officers, both local and state, are understaffed and demoralized after some short-sighted 'defund the police' motions from politicians seeking to capitalize on egregious acts by a very few officers around the country. Seattle's police are understaffed and overwhelmed keeping order and investigating the worst violent crimes."

"The best I could do is to examine financial records you subpoena with a court order," suggested Dave.

Bethany resumed her dour professional demeanor. "Two problems with that. We don't know whose records to subpoena. And, even if we did, we'd need plausible probable cause. 'I have a hunch,' isn't sufficient. Without something more concrete, getting a warrant or even contacting government agencies would simply waste their time."

"So, how could I possibly help you?" Dave asked.

"Tara told us that you and Katie are adept at discovering suspects and providing probable cause," answered Casey.

"The defense attorney in the Stegall fraud case even alluded to you being amateur sleuths," added Bethany. "Quite competent ones, I discovered while researching you."

Katie surprised them all by spontaneously volunteering, "I'll help you." She looked pointedly at Dave.

"I'm willing to review records," he responded, albeit with a reluctant voice.

"Count us in," Denyse said while gesturing to herself and Jeremy. She handed Casey a napkin with their phone numbers and email addresses while Jeremy nodded.

"Denyse and Jeremy helped break up a human trafficking ring Down Under. And they played key roles stopping an extortion operation by a white supremacy organization in Alabama," Katie explained.

"Summertime is slow at our accounting firm in Mobile," Jeremy added.

Denyse said, "I have the summer off from teaching."

"So where do we begin?" asked Katie.

Dave thought to himself, *No good deed goes unpunished.* Then he shook his head. "So, you've all decided?" After Katie, Denyse, and Jeremy nodded, he continued with a smile, "Consider your children, Denyse. What would you do with them if you and Jeremy are busy chasing leads?"

"My sister-in-law Sandra works in a day-care center and is at the end of her university term in

Australia. She would love to visit America and would gladly help care for the kids if we paid for her airline ticket. Her younger sister Sveta has found a steady boyfriend, a good lad, and won't want to leave. My brother Trevor might come."

"Why don't we invite Dingo and Beatrice too?" said Dave in exasperation, speaking of Denyse's colorful parents.

Denyse didn't notice Dave's tone. "I don't think so. Not yet, anyway."

Dave looked at Jeremy, who spoke before Dave could complain. "Dad, you know that our partner Herschel and administrator Dorothy can run Parker and Associates during the summer."

"But it isn't fair to make Herschel do all the work while we receive profits from the partnership."

Jeremy considered that. "You're right. We could pro-rate the extra days we spend away as part of the year and give Herschel that fraction of our partnerships." He looked at Denyse, who nodded.

Dave rubbed his face. "Or we could offer Herschel equivalent days off in addition to his vacation."

After a silence, Katie repeated, "So where do we begin?"

Dave sighed and looked from Bethany to Casey. "Okay. We'll finish the week of vacation our family had planned in Washington while you two collect whatever leads and suspicions you have to give us a start. That will allow Sandra time to come as well. Then we'll meet again and go over what you have. We'll follow up on anything that looks promising."

Bethany and Casey looked at each other with delight. Bethany spoke first. "But this needs to be hush-hush. My office would frown on me running a personal investigation. We'll only go to higher authorities if we discover probable cause." Then Bethany's face showed embarrassment. "Please also remember that I am an attorney working for Seattle. I'll need you to all sign this form stating that you are volunteering and expect no remuneration from the city. Even you, Casey." She looked directly at Dave. "Your compensation from Seattle was scheduled to end tomorrow anyway." She produced forms from the attaché case and collected signatures.

As she signed, Denyse kidded Bethany. "Do you know you have a split personality? You're a fun person who can switch into no-nonsense in an instant."

"I'm a lawyer, aren't I?" Bethany retorted then explained, "You can't get convictions if juries think you're frivolous."

Dave belly laughed. "You're not going to bill us for *your* services on this case, are you?"

"Only if you don't produce," Bethany quipped back.

"I need to be cautious too. I don't want to raise false hopes among my blog followers," said Casey. "Donations to my nonprofit are already dismal. Negative publicity could kill me." Then he joined the fun, "So I'll need each of you to sign a form promising that you *will* pay me."

After the laughter subsided, Katie concluded, "Then we're all set."

Katelyn and David had fallen asleep. "Jeremy and I need to get these kids in bed," said Denyse.

Chapter Four

A young woman sat alone at her university's student-center food court. She reviewed her engineering textbook in preparation for the last exam of that term. Unlike most of her classmates, Sandra had not stayed up late cramming for the final. *I've been studying all term and know this stuff,* she assured herself.

She watched as male/female pairs of students sat eating, talking, and laughing. *If God had made me look like Sveta,* she thought, *I could attract male friends.* Sandra re-looked at her textbook. *I wanted a career and good job in order to take care of my children in case something happened to my husband, like what happened to Poppa.* She remembered the hungry and cold months the remaining family had endured as war refugees after her father's death. *A good job won't be necessary if I never have any children.*

Sandra sighed. Internally she acknowledged that Sveta, youngest and impossibly pretty, had been even her Poppa's favorite. *I should have returned to Ukraine with Mama. Most twenty-one-year-old farm girls are already married there.*

She recalled the letter received from her mother after proposing her return. "Don't come back here, my sweet daughter," her mother had written. "Make a better life for yourself in Australia."

If only Poppa hadn't been killed.

Sandra's cell phone buzzed. *Why would Denyse be calling me?*

* * *

"Look at this," Denyse suggested after she and Jeremy had put Katelyn and David to bed and she had phoned Sandra offering a trip to America.

Jeremy leaned over Denyse's laptop. "It's from Casey."

"Right. He's recommending that we visit the eastern shore of Puget Sound, Kitsap County, and the Olympic Peninsula while he and Bethany collect some leads."

"Since we're on our own dollar starting tomorrow, how about googling up reasonably priced hotels there."

"Here's a former convention center, now a Baymont, in Bremerton right on the motorway."

"Looks nice enough."

Denyse and Jeremy looked up as Dave and Katie entered the suite they shared, stepping quietly to avoid waking the children.

"Look, Dad. We can afford two separate rooms starting tomorrow."

"Fine," Dave said. "As long as the kids stay with you."

Katie made a face. "Grumpy here is perturbed because he wanted to start exploring the Oregon Trail. Your father and I can take care of our grandchildren some days and nights so you two can enjoy some time together."

Denyse's face lit up with gratitude.

Dave looked at the Baymont's website. "Could be a good choice. And as I remember, a naval shipyard that played an important role in the Second World War is in Bremerton. Can you make a reservation for two rooms starting tomorrow night?"

"Probably." After a minute, Denyse announced, "Done! But we can't check in until four."

"Good work." Dave pulled out the business card Casey had provided. "Can we also look at Casey's website?"

"Sure." With a few taps, Denyse pulled up Casey's website. All the Parkers leaned in to look.

Jeremy described what he saw. "Looks like Casey regularly posts news and issues of interest to outdoors people. He publishes followers' descriptions of outdoor adventures and where-to-go tips along with photos. There's a calendar of non-commercial outdoor activities, including periodic group excursions organized by Casey. I see reposted notices from parks and the DFW." After a moment of silence, Jeremy concluded, "This site is well done."

Denyse pointed to a spot on the screen. "That's why Casey has 13,141 followers."

"That *is* impressive," Dave admitted.

After examining Casey's website, Katie started, "So now we have several days of vacation before Bethany and Casey give us any leads. What shall we do tomorrow until we can check in to the Baymont?"

Denyse spoke first. "I looked at a pamphlet in this hotel's lobby for whale watching. I've always wanted to see a whale." Without being asked, she googled to find a service. "On the west side of Puget Sound, Port Townsend is our best bet."

Katie looked at the others. "Whale watching tomorrow okay with everyone?"

"Make the reservations," said Dave. "Here's my credit card for everybody."

Katie continued, "Then the day after tomorrow and the next, I'll watch the children while Jeremy and Denyse take our rental SUV and go wherever they want."

Jeremy and Denyse looked at each other with joy. "Anywhere you say, my beloved," said Denyse.

"I'd like to see Mount Rainier."

"You mean the active volcano?"

"It isn't erupting right now. And it's in a national park."

"I suppose."

"What about me?" Dave interjected.

"You can use my computer to study up on this area's history and geography then visit Bremerton," Katie suggested.

Dave visibly perked up.

"Mom, you're something special," said Jeremy.

"Just don't you forget that."

Fifty-six rough-looking men and half that many equally tough women of various ages gathered in a barn. Nearly all attending wore camouflage clothes and army-style boots. Most carried holstered sidearms. A few men carried automatic rifles across their backs. The crowd buzzed with the comradery of people with a purpose. Camping gear and food supplies brought by the group had been stacked in piles around the barn walls.

A man came into the barn through a side door and shouted, "Attention!"

The men and women froze in various styles of erect posture. A short, stocky, clean-shaven man of about fifty entered through the side door followed by two lieutenants. The three climbed wooden steps to a rough platform that held an American flag and a podium. They stood facing the flag.

"Ready, salute!" the stocky man commanded in a gruff voice. All those present raised their hands to their foreheads. "I pledge allegiance to the flag of the United States of America . . ." At the conclusion of the pledge, he ordered, "At ease."

Most present began cheering and shouting slogans: "Renew pioneer spirit! Reclaim our rights! Live free or die!"

Their leader approached the podium and waited for the tumult to die down. "We're here to bring true meaning back to our flag and live independently, the way our forbearers intended. All that is within America belongs to you—you who have joined the heritage of patriots who fought and died for this land. They fought the British who enslaved them and Indians who killed innocent men, women, and children. The pioneers only wanted to live free. Now we stand against the Eastern bureaucracies which have taken over government at every level and want to dictate how you will live."

The listeners erupted in spontaneous approval of those words.

After a minute of noise, the leader spoke again. "We're here to prepare. Tomorrow we'll have live-fire drills and practice maneuvers." He indicated the two men behind him. "These officers won't make the day easy for you. Get some rest tonight. We start at dawn."

The leader stepped back. One of his two subordinates shouted, "Let's hear it for our captain!" The group roared with acclamation. Their captain left the platform and mingled with the militia, shaking hands and slapping backs. Loud patriotic music from a speaker filled the barn.

Chapter Five

"We're crossing the Hood Canal," Dave announced while driving to Port Townsend the next morning. "This floating bridge sank in an eighty-five-mile-per-hour storm in 1979."

Jeremy, seated in the front and knowing his father's love of factual history, prompted him further. "Why did they use a floating bridge, Dad?"

"Well, Hood Canal is a one-and-a-half-mile-wide fjord and three hundred and forty feet deep here. It was created by the same ice-age continental glacier that formed the Puget Sound."

"Did the glacier gouge the fjord out?"

The science teacher in Katie emerged. "Partly. But a sheet of ice a mile or more thick is heavy. About 13,000 years ago, the glacier pressed an indention into the Earth's crust like it did Puget Sound. Gradually, the Earth's crust is bouncing back."

"What else noteworthy is nearby?" asked Denyse from the back seat.

"Well, the Bangor naval base is just a few miles that way." Dave pointed to the south. "That's the home port for many of America's ballistic missile submarines."

"You mean the submarines are kept there in case of a war?" asked Denyse.

"No, ballistic submarines spend most of their time quietly on the move, hiding in the ocean. That way a surprise nuclear attack can't destroy them. Their ability to strike back is our primary deterrent to a first strike."

"What are all those gorgeous tall light purple and white flowers on stalks?" asked Denyse.

"Those are foxgloves," Katie answered. "I've never seen so many. Sometimes you see them in Alabama gardens. They are apparently wild here and obviously prolific. The dark pink flowers you see in patches alongside the road are called fireweed. They grow in the Northern states and Canada at mid to low elevations."

* * *

The Parkers stood in the stern of the whale-watching boat admiring the snow-covered Olympic

Mountains on the western and southern horizons. "The mountains are being formed by the Juan de Fuca tectonic plate sliding under North America," Katie explained. "The Olympics are actually debris scraped off its top surface."

"I've never seen anything more magnificent," said Denyse.

Jeremy agreed, "Me neither. But Puget Sound is pretty special by itself. Look at this clear, clean water. It makes our muddy Mobile Bay look dirty. It's calm like Mobile Bay, though."

The boat's tour guide and whale expert overheard Jeremy. "Looks can be deceiving. As the tide goes out, forty cubic miles of water in the Puget Sound moves toward the ocean. Once the tide turns, the water doesn't stop instantly, so water coming in and water still going out form rivers not evident by the tranquil surface. Sometimes we see whirlpools where in and out rivers pass one another."

The boat slowed. "A gray whale is on our right," announced the captain through the intercom. "By Washington law, we have to remain two hundred yards away from any whale."

Tourists crowded the starboard side with cameras and binoculars. Katie momentarily thought, *We could capsize with everybody on one side.* But the boat, ballasted for tourists, barely listed.

Jeremy held Katelyn on his shoulder to help her see. She pointed and said, "He's looking at us."

Indeed the whale did appear to look at the boat through an eye that seemed tiny compared to its massive body. A murmured "Oooh" came from the spectators as the whale spouted a spray of water, took a breath through its back, and dived, exposing its tail flukes for a couple of seconds.

Katie, holding David, tried to point out the whale. But a flock of hovering seagulls diverted the little boy's attention.

As the boat slowly paralleled the whale's direction of travel, the tour guide explained, "Gray whales migrate during March through May from Baja, California—where their calves are born—to Alaska. But fifteen are known to remain year-round in the Strait of Juan de Fuca between Washington and British Columbia. This whale is one of those."

"What do gray whales eat?" asked Denyse.

"Their diet is mostly bottom-dwelling crustaceans but also schooling fishes, shrimp, and seafloor worms," responded the guide.

Suddenly, the voice of the boat's captain returned, "Folks, a pod of orcas has been spotted by a Canadian tour out of Victoria about thirty minutes from here. Shall we go see them?"

General applause answered affirmatively. "Please take your seats," asked the captain. After all had found seats, the boat accelerated until it was bouncing over the choppy water.

Twenty-seven minutes later a flotilla of small, slow-moving boats appeared. Their boat decelerated and joined the others. "Watch on our left or port side," said the guide.

Squeals of joy came from the tourists as a black and white head emerged from the water and looked around. The orca then hurried to catch up with several others visible by their vertical fins and backs breaking surface. "Orcas can see and hear well above water," explained their guide. "That one was probably getting a bearing or maybe listening for barking sea lions." She went on, "Seventy-three orcas live permanently in Washington's waters. We call them 'residents.' Unfortunately, several of these haven't been spotted for nearly a year. Our residents' diet is exclusively fish, particularly salmon. But this pod spends most of its time in Alaska and hunts other mammals."

"How do you know that?" Katie asked.

Their guide held up a set of laminated cards showing orcas. "Every orca has a different pattern of white and black skin. Each animal can be identified by their markings. One of the other boats identified these orcas as being what we call a transient pod."

"And they eat seals?" Denyse guessed.

"This pod, yes. Sea lions climb onto rocks for safety. Gray whales sometimes hide in kelp beds. Porpoises listen carefully and try to swim away from marauding orcas."

"I guess that's why they're called 'killer whales.'"

"They can be killers. But orcas aren't really whales. They're actually a large type of dolphin. And the males are mama's boys. They remain with their mother until one of them dies."

Katelyn pointed. "I see a big bird. He must be old because his head is white like Granddad's."

Everybody looked where she pointed to see a bird effortlessly soaring over the water. "That's a bald eagle," explained their guide. "At about one year, their head feathers become white. This one might be following the orcas hoping they'll kill something to eat and leave scraps. Our Department of Fish and Wildlife estimates we have about four thousand in Washington, mostly near Puget Sound."

* * *

"I really enjoyed seeing the whales and eagles," said Denyse as they walked down Port Townsend's Water Street. She looked around. "These are big, beautiful buildings for such a small town."

Taking that as his pedantic cue, Dave explained. "In the 1800s, the harbor here was very busy. Sailing ships could maneuver in easier than into Seattle or Tacoma's tight waters. Many people thought Port Townsend would become the biggest seaport on the West Coast. Speculators built these Victorian buildings, creating an economic boom. Then the financial panic of 1893 dried up capital. At the same time, larger engine-powered ships found Seattle and Tacoma more convenient. Finally, the railroads declined extending their lines from Tacoma to here. The triple whammy turned boom into bust. Port Townsend nearly turned into a ghost town."

"How did the town survive?"

"In 1896, the US Army came to the remote Pacific Northwest. They built massive artillery fortifications as part of the coastal defense system.

Fort Worden in Port Townsend defended the entire Salish Sea, of which Puget Sound is part. Most strategically, Fort Worden protected the Puget Sound Naval Shipyard which had been established in Bremerton—where we are staying—in 1891."

Katie had heard enough history and changed the conversation. "I'd like to try this place for a late lunch." She pointed at a restaurant featuring a 1950s motif. Inside, the Parkers found a black and white tile floor, a stool-lined fountain bar, old-fashioned booths, and a jukebox playing Elvis.

Sitting in a booth, Dave ordered the Fried Egg Diner Classic. The others followed with burgers and fries in baskets and corn dogs for Katelyn and David.

"I also want a vintage American milkshake," added Denyse.

After taking a bus and light-rail public transport from Olympia into Seattle, Casey waited for Bethany outside the courtroom where she had endured a tedious day listening to victim statements after the Stegall conviction. He saw her walk stoically out carrying a briefcase. "You look like you've had a hard day."

"You can't even imagine hour after hour of sad stories. Older couples describing the loss of their savings while Stegall's two lawyers sit there making two hundred dollars an hour each for stifling yawns."

Casey shook his head. "Are we still on for dinner?"

"Any place that serves liquor."

"I know a sports bar in walking distance that serves great burgers and onion rings."

Fifteen minutes later Casey nursed a beer while Bethany sipped a double-sized margarita. "Ah, that's better," she said.

"Have you found any good leads for the Parkers?" asked Casey.

"A couple. I searched police reports today while the judge received a transfusion of caffeine. How about you?"

"I've got a query out to my blog followers. I'm flooded with complaints about everything anybody doesn't like in Washington."

"I'm not surprised."

After ordering burgers with onion rings, they sat in silence for a minute. "I was hoping we might go on a hike or something this weekend."

"Casey, I . . . I've got work to catch up on. I'm sorry."

"That's okay." Casey couldn't hide his disappointment. "Maybe I could keep your pencils sharpened or something."

Bethany looked hard at him. "After eating, we could go to my apartment for an hour, if that's what you want."

"That sounds enticing, but it's not what I meant. I love you, Bethany, and just want to spend more time with you."

"The time we have together is good, Casey. I've got an important job—"

"I was hoping for more commitment."

"How can I be more committed? Aren't we lovers?"

"There's more to a relationship than sex."

Bethany drained her large margarita and shrugged.

"Are you interested in getting married to anyone again ever?" asked Casey.

Their burgers came. "Please package mine to go," Bethany told the waiter and pulled out a credit card.

"I'll pay," insisted Casey.

Bethany handed the card to the waiter. "For both of us. And add twenty percent for yourself."

"Bethany, I just wanted—"

"Another time, Casey. I'm tired." The waiter returned with a to-go bag and a charge printout to sign. Bethany collected her things and left.

* * *

Aaron Wierzbowski rang a doorbell in a suburb of Olympia. A tired young woman opened the door. "Hi, Mary. How are you and the kids doing?"

The late-twenties mother stepped outside her modest home, leaving the front door ajar. A girl of five and her younger brother of three peered out. "Not great, Aaron. It's been ten months now. I'm facing the reality of being alone. Trying to maintain a routine for the kids. Have you heard anything, anything at all?"

"No, I haven't. The state police and I have followed up every lead, and there's a national bulletin out. Nobody has given up, but there's nothing left to go on. We're just hoping for a break. But I promise to not rest until I find Hal."

Mary sighed. "It's hard not having closure." She gestured toward her children. "I know Hal would never desert us. He isn't alive. We're out of money too. The state can't pay someone who hasn't reported for work. The insurance won't settle without a declaration of death, which a court won't grant for seven years. I've looked for a job, but the wage hardly covers the cost of childcare. Next week we're leaving Washington to live with my parents in Boise. They're not well off financially either. But it's a free roof, and they'll help with the kids. I should be able to get some sort of job. We can't sell this house without Hal's signature. But we hope to rent it furnished for enough to cover the monthly payments."

Aaron handed her a check. "We took up a collection at DFW. Hal was a good officer and well liked."

Mary looked at the check. "Eight thousand dollars?" She started to cry and hugged Aaron. "I can't believe it. This will help a lot. Thank everybody for me."

"No problem. Do you need help moving?"

"My parents are coming with a U-Haul trailer. We could use help loading on Saturday."

"I'll be here." Aaron nodded at Mary and turned to go back to his car.

"Hal looked up to you, Aaron," Mary called after him.

Her words only compounded Aaron's feelings of helplessness, frustration, and determination.

Chapter Six

"I never imagined being so close to such a massive snow-covered mountain," said Denyse as she and Jeremy hiked a park-service trail on the lower slopes of Mount Rainier.

"This is pretty awesome," Jeremy agreed. "But you mean volcano."

Denyse playfully grimaced. "Don't remind me."

"Then you don't want to hear about the eruption of Mount Saint Helens in 1980? Fifty-seven people died."

"Where is this Saint Helens volcano?"

"About fifty-five miles south of here. But Mount Saint Helens gave plenty of warning tremors. Most of those killed had refused to evacuate. Interestingly, in case of a volcanic eruption of a snow-covered mountain, you might survive by climbing to higher ground."

Denyse stopped to stare at her husband. "Why higher ground?"

Jeremy turned toward Denyse. "The volcano's heat can melt the ice and cause a flood."

"And how would you know all this?"

"I read about it in the visitor center. And here's another surprise."

"What?"

"The term 'flying saucer' for UFO originated at Mount Rainier."

"You're kidding."

"In 1947, a civilian pilot reported seeing saucer-like objects, glowing and flying at high speeds. Later scientific investigations proved that mountain air oscillations can create cloud formations that look remarkably like saucers." Jeremy showed his wife a photo in a park service handout showing clouds that uncannily resembled UFOs.

Jeremy is Dave and Katie's son, the result of a history-buff father and a science-teacher mother, realized Denyse.

She resumed the hike until she paused before a wide field of tall blueish-purple wildflowers. "Look at those gorgeous flowers growing completely wild. I've always loved wildflowers. They give beauty freely to everyone without asking anything in return. First the foxgloves and fireweed. What are these?"

"Those are lupines," responded Jeremy after consulting the guide he had picked up in the park's visitor center.

"I feel like I've been transported into a different world. I've never seen wildflowers growing profusely in so many colors and shapes . . . look! What is that?" She pointed to a brown animal munching some of the flowers.

Jeremy used his camera to zoom closer before snapping a picture. "That's a marmot. They're closely related to our Southern woodchucks. Both are actually a big type of squirrel."

"You mean like the bushy-tailed gray squirrels in our backyard trees in Alabama?"

"That's what Mom told me as a boy. And she was a science teacher."

"Well, marmots look like Australian wombats." When Jeremy didn't comment, Denyse asked, "Why does your father call squirrels 'tree rats'?"

"Because squirrels are rodents like rats, I suppose. But Dad likes squirrels. He puts food out for them and the birds in winter."

They watched the marmot until it lazily shambled away. A few hundred yards later they climbed over a large snowbank from the previous winter blocking the trail. "Take a picture of me standing here in the snow with the mountain in the background," suggested Denyse. "My family Down Under won't believe snow remaining in mid-summer."

Jeremy nodded. "Many people in south Alabama would be equally surprised."

Denyse then broached an upcoming choice. "Speaking of Alabama, have you decided what you'll do this fall?"

Jeremy shook his head. "I'm afraid I'd neglect the accounting firm if I were to win office in the legislature. That wouldn't be fair to Dad and Herschel or to you and the kids."

"Being a state senator isn't a full-time job, and Montgomery is only two hours from Mobile. Everybody will be fine in your absences. But you also need to consider that with your talent and popularity, this would probably lead to higher offices."

"Think so?"

Denyse smiled. "I certainly do. There's nothing to limit you."

Jeremy changed the subject. "Let's get a picture of you in the snow."

After posing against the snow wearing shorts, Denyse commented, "Your parents are always wonderful to us. But them insisting on our taking the SUV for an excursion while they care for Katelyn and David sets a new high."

"Good thing Dad selected an SUV big enough for all six of us."

"And Sandra when she comes."

Jeremy nodded agreement. "Dad is probably exploring Bremerton right now. The naval base there played a key role in World War Two. He'll be happy studying local history today."

Dave stood staring at the USS *Nimitz*, named after America's naval commander in the Pacific during World War II. Although massive, the aircraft carrier based in Bremerton seemed small to carry up to a hundred and thirty jets and be home for over six thousand sailors on a half-year deployment.

Dave frowned while reviewing a history of Washington's participation in World War II. The University of Washington's football team had played a game in Honolulu on Dec 6th, 1941. Following the Japanese surprise attack the following morning, the army had come to their hotel, passed out rifles, and put the football players on the beach to fight an anticipated invasion. *I'll bet those boys were scared witless*, he thought.

The naval shipyard seemed quiet even though a dozen ships were receiving service or upgrades. Dave's mind transported him in time as he thought about the desperate around-the-clock work of shipfitters and Rosie Riveters supporting the war in the Pacific following Pearl Harbor. *In some respects, the Pacific war was fought right here by men and women not in the military.* Dave choked with emotion as he remembered battleships sunk at

Pearl Harbor on December 7th. Except for the *Arizona*, they had been floated, hastily patched, and towed to Bremerton to be repaired and sent back to the war. He imagined scenes involving the barrage balloons hung over the harbor, massive search lights, and batteries of anti-aircraft guns to repel possible aerial attacks.

Near downtown he toured the Puget Sound Navy Museum, which featured life on a carrier. Before leaving he commented to one of the volunteer attendants, "When I saw the *Nimitz*, there weren't any jets."

The man about Dave's age smiled. "The air wing is based on Whidbey Island. They fly to the *Nimitz* once it's at sea." He added, "I served on her in the eighties."

"Thank you," Dave said with respect. The former navy man nodded in acknowledgment.

After the museum, Dave wandered down the boardwalk then walked on a pier leading to a floating breakwater surrounding Bremerton's marina. He paused at the USS *Franklin* memorial where 807 sailors were honored after having died in a single 1944 kamikaze attack in addition to 117 killed in other actions. Dave then admired the ferries and other boats plying the inland waters against a background of dark evergreen forests under a blue sky. He imagined the sailing ships that had transported cargos of lumber and logs from Washington's tall, straight forests to market. His mind saw fishing boats bringing in full hulls of salmon. On a placard, he read about the mosquito fleet of small, locally built boats that had served as transportation in western Washington before roads were built.

Everyplace has a history, none richer than Washington, he thought. *I can hardly wait to follow the Oregon Trail that brought American pioneers to such a wonderful place.*

* * *

Katie sat down next to Dave on the hotel room couch as he watched local news on TV. "Katelyn and David are finally asleep."

Dave patted her knee while following a report about homeless encampments in Seattle. "You gave them such a fun day they didn't want it to end."

"Who gave them the horsey rides?" When Dave didn't respond Katie continued, "I hope Jeremy and Denyse are enjoying their cabin near Mount Rainier."

"I can guarantee it." Dave didn't take his eyes off the TV.

"I'm enjoying Washington," said Katie. "But I wish we could do something to get started on the investigation."

"Let's call Tara," Dave suggested. "She set Casey and Bethany onto us. Maybe she has something to add."

"Good idea."

Tara's husband, Jeff, answered the phone. "Tara is just getting out of the shower."

"How are you two doing?" Katie asked.

"Busy. But a world better than when I had my daughter, Sam, alone. Tara has made a great mother and is a genius at business. Thank you a million times for straightening me up about her, Dave."

"My pleasure," Dave said.

"Every few months Tara needs a week or so away by herself."

Dave expressed understanding. "More than a decade of living independently is a hard habit to break."

"Yeah. Here she is," said Jeff. "Tara, I have Dave and Katie on speaker phone."

"Hello, Dave and Katie Parker," said Tara in her husky voice.

"How are your children?" asked Katie.

"Sam is growing up. And little Katie stood up last week. Having a baby was a pain in the . . . everywhere. But Denyse was right. Little Katie is worth it all."

Tara and Katie continued talk of children until Dave broke in. "You've gotten us involved in something here, Tara."

"So, Casey and Bethany managed to recruit you? I'm glad. They're our fellow outdoors advocates. There may be problems up there. I've heard complaints about the decline of wildlife and roughnecks flaunting regulations intended to protect ecosystems. Stories about secretive groups circulating among my contacts point to something going on in Washington. I sense something bad and knew that if anybody could uncover what, it would be you two."

"What can you tell us?"

"Hard evidence to support my feelings? Nothing beyond rumors. But Casey is highly respected in our circles. If he smells smoke too, there's fire someplace."

"What about Bethany?" asked Katie.

"I first felt leery when I found out Bethany is a prosecuting attorney. Then I liked her. Bethany drove me all around looking at possible business sites. Obviously Casey adores her. But she seems to keep him at a distance. Too bad because that Casey is quite a catch. If I hadn't met Jeff—"

"You'd still be living in a camper all alone in the world," interrupted Katie.

Tara laughed. "Or maybe worse. Jeff is the best thing that ever happened to me. I didn't know what I was missing."

Dave told about Anton Stegall and the conviction Bethany secured.

"I was once a con-person too," Tara admitted.

"True," Dave agreed. "But this guy defrauded widows and charities. All you did is separate tourists from a few dollars."

"I did try to separate Jeremy from his college fund, though."

"And you didn't go through with it. Now you've changed and have become a successful businesswoman."

"You know what God says. If you invent a better mousetrap . . . you'll be waiting for your doorbell to ring while businesswomen like me are selling inferior mousetraps."

"God never said that, honey," responded Katie.

"Well, He could have, because it's true."

Chapter Seven

The following morning, Denyse spotted a billboard advertising Northwest Trek Wildlife Park as Jeremy drove back to Bremerton from Mount Rainier. She googled the park on her phone. "They have forty species of wild animals from all over the Pacific Northwest. I want you to take me there."

Jeremy glanced away from the road at the picture she held up on her phone. "Is it a zoo?"

"I think it's a hybrid between a zoo and a wild animal preserve. They have bears, wolves, and American mountain lions. Obviously they need to be confined somehow. They show non-predators living in their natural environment. People watch them from a little trolly. I visited your volcano. This is where I want to go."

"Okay. Let your phone show us the way."

"It's six miles ahead."

Inside the park, Denyse and Jeremy found predators in enclosures of more than an acre with running water and natural vegetation. Many were playing with toys provided by the park or otherwise entertaining themselves. A massive grizzly bear frolicked in a pool of clear water. Nearby a wolf sang with the joy of howling. "I've never seen wild animals so contented," said Denyse. "I love this place!"

"Surviving in the wild is a struggle for most animals," commented Jeremy. "This is like what living at a resort would be to humans."

A park attendant overheard them. "You could say these are the lucky ones. We want our animals to enjoy comfortable and happy lives."

Denyse turned to see a young woman pushing a cart laden with salmon, meat, and various fruits and vegetables to distribute. "How do you get the animals?"

"The Department of Fish and Wildlife or licensed wildlife shelters sometimes bring us animals that wouldn't survive on their own or would endanger people. Many of our animals aren't capable of surviving in the wild. They may have been permanently injured by a car. Others were orphaned and raised by humans. When a potentially dangerous animal has become accustomed to and depends on humans for food, they can't be released. Our grizzly bears are examples of that."

"What about non-dangerous animals?" asked Jeremy.

"Any wild animal can be dangerous if threatened. Our park is 725 acres, more than a square mile," the attendant answered. "We have herbivores—elk, deer, bison, mountain goats, bighorn sheep, and even a few caribou—roaming free, feeding themselves, and breeding. We provide a ride that allows you to see them in their natural habitat without disturbing them."

* * *

The next day all the Parkers waited at the Seattle/Tacoma Airport, called SeaTac, to meet Sandra. Dave asked Denyse, "Sandra is Lena's sister, right?"

"Yes. After you rescued Lena from human traffickers and brought my foolish brother Trevor home, my parents helped Lena's family immigrate to Australia from Ukraine. Their father had been killed for refusing to support the Russians who confiscated the Travnikov farm."

"Is this the sister who caused the fight that nearly sent Trevor to prison?"

"No. That was Sveta, who is beautiful like Lena. Sandra has always felt like she's in Sveta's shadow even though she's older. All the Travnikov girls lost their father, had unimaginable experiences as refugees, and moved into a vastly different English-speaking culture in Australia. Then their mother deserted them by returning to Ukraine and marrying a widowed pastor. Sandra has been through a lot."

After a poignant pause, Denyse added, "Sandra's twenty-one years old but seems younger. My parents are paying for her to attend Uni. She's a second-year engineering student."

"But Sandra knows how to care for children?"

"Plenty enough. Like Lena, she cared for younger Travnikov children and later worked in Lena's daycare business." Denyse pointed at a plain but not unpleasant-looking young woman exiting immigration. She was wearing a homemade dress with a backpack and carrying an old-fashioned non-roller suitcase. "There she is."

* * *

Sandra felt bewildered in the chaos of a busy American airport and simply followed signs saying EXIT. Emerging from passport control, she found a crowd of people looking in her direction. She recognized one smiling face. *Denyse!*

Denyse approached and gave her a prolonged hug before stepping back. "Thank you for coming, Sandra. Welcome to the United States."

"I am happy to be here."

Denyse gestured to a group of friendly-looking Americans. "These are the Parkers."

Sandra saw an attractive and distinguished older couple who smiled at her. "This is Dave and Katie, my father-in-law and mother-in-law," Denyse explained. "And here is my husband, Jeremy."

Sandra thought, *Dave and Katie saved Lena and rescued Trevor, who talks about and admires Jeremy.* While Denyse introduced her children, Katelyn and David, Sandra could not help thinking, *Unlike me, everybody in this family looks like movie stars.* She felt in awe of the Parkers.

After hugs all around, Sandra admired the children and produced gifts from her backpack—a book about Australian animals for Katelyn and a stuffed kangaroo toy for David.

Jeremy picked up her suitcase. "This way."

While leaving the airport, everybody asked questions about Sandra's long flight and family back in Australia. She answered, "They all wanted to come, even Sveta. But she has a boyfriend. An Australian Lena approves of."

Their route took them through Tacoma, which Sandra looked at with curiosity. Then they passed over the Tacoma Narrows Bridge. "I know about this famous bridge," she said. "The bridge fell down in a small wind because of dynamic instability. They show us a film in engineering school. The lesson to every student is, 'Don't mess up.'"

"How did they build the new bridge differently, Sandra?" asked Katie.

"The new bridge uses suspension cables to support a stiff truss."

"Sandra has very good marks in engineering school," Denyse explained.

"That is because I am good in maths. But I am between terms now and would even sit out a semester for the chance to see America."

"Is anybody but me ready for lunch?" asked Dave.

"Count me in," responded Katie. "The next exit is Gig Harbor, which I read is rather picturesque in a New England fashion. Could we eat there?"

With general approval, Jeremy steered off of Highway 16 and drove into a little town. The main street followed the shore of a small port off Puget Sound with trendy shops on each side. Docks for fishing and pleasure boats lined the shore. Sandra internally marveled at the casually dressed but obviously well-off people on the sidewalks.

"This is charming. Just like a picture," said Denyse. She googled up a highly rated seafood restaurant overlooking the harbor and directed Jeremy to it. Once they parked and had been seated, a waitress delivered menus and drinks.

"Try the ahi poke," Jeremy challenged his father.

"I like tuna, but not raw in soy sauce," Dave returned before ordering fried calamari.

Katie ordered a crab BLT and warm bread pudding for dessert.

Sandra's heart quailed at the prices, thinking, *This will take all the money I have.*

Denyse, sitting next to Sandra, noticed her looking at the soups and whispered, "Dave will pick up the check, honey. Order anything you like. I'm having the broiled salmon and asparagus plus a cup of clam chowder."

Nevertheless, Sandra's tongue froze when the waitress asked her choice. Denyse intervened, "Why don't you try what I'm having, Sandra?"

Sandra nodded. Privately, she thought, *I don't belong here with these people. I'll just sit quietly.* Then she saw Denyse make eye contact with Jeremy across the table and then almost imperceptibly tilt her head indicating, "Talk to Sandra."

Immediately, Jeremy began asking about her experiences as a new resident in Australia. Having lived there himself, he had plenty of humorous observations of Aussie culture. Sandra laughed as Jeremy told about the ruckus Denyse's father, Dingo, created at their wedding and the black eye Dave had received. Denyse rolled her eyes while continuing to smile.

Sandra started to relax.

Their orders arrived. Sandra tasted the salmon, grilled and basted with fresh lemon juice and herbs. The taste and tenderness nearly took her breath away. The asparagus, broiled after being dipped into olive oil and seasoned with garlic, was no less delicious.

She heard Jeremy still making conversation. "Sandra, what have you observed in Washington so far?"

"I am only just come. But the evergreen trees, they are enormous. This place looks like the *Twilight* vampire movies."

Jeremy responded, "Good observation. Those movies were made here in Washington. Would you like to go see a vampire?"

"You mean a real vampire?"

"Sure. They keep a few in bat cages at the Seattle zoo."

Denyse spoke to Sandra, "Honey, don't you listen to this scoundrel. He is playing with you."

Jeremy tried to look repentant. "Well, I never had a little sister to tease."

Then Denyse added, "Seattle doesn't have any vampires. They stay in the Hoh Rainforest."

Sandra smiled. "Well, I wouldn't want to marry one, anyway."

Dave broke into their merriment to say, "Tomorrow is America's Fourth-of-July national holiday. We celebrate winning our independence from England. Denyse, can you find us a good place to show Sandra fireworks?"

The next day, Sandra stood with the Parkers on a pier extending into the Puget Sound. Bright fireworks erupted from hundreds of places all along the dark tree-lined shoreline in every direction. She heard *Ooohs* and *Ahhs* from the Parkers.

"I'm glad you arrived in time to see this," Dave said to Sandra.

But to Denyse, Sandra seemed somber. "Do you like the fireworks, Sandra?" she asked quietly.

"The booms and flashes of light. They remind me of the war in Ukraine. Noise and explosions all along the horizon, like here, but they were getting closer to us. After the Russians killed my father . . . Mama took us and we run west to get away."

"I'm sorry, honey. Would you like to go back to the hotel?"

"No, this is special to Americans. Please do not tell them not special to me."

Chapter Eight

At seven the evening of July 5th, Katie saw a gray SUV pull into the Baymont parking lot from her hotel window. Bethany got out of the driver's side and retrieved a stack of manila folders from the rear seat. Casey exited the passenger side with his knapsack. They headed toward the hotel's lobby without speaking. "They're here," she told Dave. "I'll go down and meet them. Tell Denyse and Jeremy, and then come down and join us."

Katie found Bethany and Casey waiting apart from each other in silence. Bethany, apparently in her professional demeanor and wearing courtroom attire including makeup, cradled the folders in one arm. Casey stood awkwardly nearby. Katie shook hands with each. "We're excited to see what you have for us."

Dave, along with Jeremy and Denyse, came down the elevator from their rooms on the top floor. Once in the lobby, he greeted Bethany and Casey and pointed down a hallway. "I've reserved a meeting room for us."

In the meeting room, Bethany placed her stack of folders on the table and took a seat.

Casey fumbled with his knapsack and pulled out a thick stack of printed emails and Facebook posts. "These are responses to a query I made to my blog followers." He grinned sheepishly. "Believe me. I culled out the most trivial ones."

* * *

Katie waited for her husband to take charge. "Alright, let's start with Casey's leads," Dave suggested and picked up Casey's pile of pages. "If you find anything interesting, speak up," he said while distributing a handful to each participant except Casey.

Sounds of shuffling papers and an occasional *mmm* created a low buzz in the room while Casey fidgeted. Katie noticed him frequently glancing at Bethany, who studied pages with intense concentration. *Casey looks a little crestfallen. He calls Bethany his girlfriend. I wonder if she calls him her boyfriend?*

Dave spoke first. "Here's one about sea lions disappearing near Bainbridge Island."

Bethany commented without looking up. "That could be because of transient orcas from Alaska. They've been spotted in that area several times this summer."

The low buzz returned until Jeremy snickered. "A sasquatch has been reported near Forks. That's where they filmed the vampire movies. Maybe Sasquatch drinks blood."

Nobody commented.

"Here's a complaint about an increase in forest fires," offered Denyse.

Casey appeared grateful for any opportunity to speak. "Maybe exacerbated by global warming. But some of my environmentalist blog followers blame everything on global warming."

"I've got a complaint about crowded communal camping areas in the parks," said Dave. "I'll put this one with those blaming littering on out-of-state tourists."

"Here's one reporting eagle feathers found near a discarded shotgun shell," said Jeremy.

Denyse reacted in surprise. "Hunters?"

"My wife is an animal lover," Jeremy explained. "All us Parkers are to some degree."

"I am too," responded Casey. "But some of my most loyal followers are responsible hunters. And without the wolves and grizzly bears of earlier times, deer and elk populations need controlling."

"Why don't you release tigers?" Jeremy's expression revealed that he was teasing.

Casey played along with a smile. "That might control human population too." Then he became serious. "Damage one part of an ecosystem and you affect all parts."

Bethany held up an email. "Here's a hiker insisting that he is seeing less wildlife. The ones he sees appear more wary than usual. He hasn't seen a bear all summer."

"Aren't animals in parks usually less wary?" Dave asked.

"I guess that makes the neighborhood where we live in Alabama a park," quipped Denyse. "Goodness knows the nearly tame deer are pests there."

"Maybe if you wouldn't feed them?" Jeremy teased.

Denyse looked at her husband with a smile. "And who puts the corn out when I forget?"

Katie called the group back to business by saying, "Here's a Facebook post of tree stumps in a restricted area."

"Likely tree rustlers," suggested Bethany.

Dave held up three sheets. "Here are three complaints from fishermen that salmon and steelhead catches are down."

"That's a pretty routine complaint here in Washington. There are thirty-two recognized Indian tribes in Washington, each a sovereign nation. By a court ruling, American Indians are entitled to fifty percent of the catch. European-origin fishers and the Indians frequently blame each other. Probably they both cheat sometimes on their quotas," explained Casey.

"Here's a camper who found a dead and mutilated bear in the Olympic National Park," said Denyse.

"I've got one like that too. Except in the Olympic National Forest," added Bethany.

"Thank you, Casey," said Dave. "We can try to follow up on the most promising tips by contacting the senders and asking for more details."

"I'll interview Sasquatch," Jeremy volunteered.

Denyse gave her husband a stern behave-yourself look.

"Now let's look at Bethany's reports," suggested Katie.

"Well, I don't have as many potential leads. But mine are from law enforcement records." Rather than pass out her numbered folders, Bethany picked up each and described the contents.

"Number one: Hikers and campers have found and reported four small animal live traps on government lands this year. The DFW confiscated each trap.

"Number two: Three resident and fairly young orcas have disappeared. Since orcas have no natural predators and remain with their pods, this is unusual.

"Number three: The DFW has issued twenty percent more citations for fishing in restricted waters as compared to the previous high.

"Number four: Environmental citations for unauthorized chemical waste are up thirty percent.

"Number five: A University of Washington tracking collar from black bear forty-two was found recently in a dumpster near Sequim."

Jeremy interrupted before Bethany went on. "How would a tracking collar end up in a dumpster?"

Casey speculated, "Probably somebody killed the bear accidently, perhaps by a car, or maybe on purpose. Then they cut off and discarded the collar without realizing that scientists could still track it."

"What could have happened to the bear's body?" asked Denyse.

"Whether accidently or on purpose, the killer might have wanted the skin," answered Casey. "And some people really like bear meat. It's frequently and legally served at private wild-game dinners."

Bethany nodded before continuing, "Number six and the last of mine: A DFW officer, Hal Dulfer, disappeared last summer. He was last seen patrolling for fishermen who exceeded the two-fish limit or used barbed treble hooks along the Sol Duc River near Olympic National Park. No trace of him or his car has been found. This probably doesn't relate to our investigation. Cars are periodically discovered in lakes or ravines with accident victims."

"Was that a state vehicle or a personal car?" asked Dave.

"He was driving an official DFW car that day." Bethany shrugged. "I suppose he could have even run away somewhere. That would be unusual because he was married and had two young children. But stranger things have happened."

Dave exhaled. "Whew! There's a lot here. And still not much to go on."

Katie added, "There are logical possibilities to answer most leads. Wildlife populations can cycle. Cougars, orcas, and eagles take more prey as their populations increase."

"But you will take a few days to check these out?" asked Bethany.

Dave saw Bethany and Casey's hopeful yet anxious expressions. He looked at Katie, Denyse, and Jeremy. "Let's divide these up and then start making some calls. Maybe something will turn up."

"I'll start with the tracking collar," volunteered Katie.

* * *

Dr. Collins, a zoology professor at the University of Washington in Seattle, explained, "Bear forty-two was a sow with a pair of cubs. We had seen the cubs during the previous winter when we inserted a camera into her den. I had two graduate students tracking her by GPS to determine how her habits and patterns varied compared to the previous year when she had no cubs."

Katie nodded. "What did they discover?"

"My students discovered that animal research is unpredictable. The loss of forty-two set their PhD dissertations back at least a year."

Katie grimaced to signal regret, but persisted, "Did they find out anything about the bear's habits or favorite locations?"

"Probably. But the research wasn't conclusive. Why do you want to know?"

Katie gestured to Dave, Denyse, Jeremy, and Casey, who stood nearby listening. "We're trying to discover if the bear's death was accidental or deliberate."

Professor Collins thought for a minute. "Why not give you what we have?" He picked up his office phone and punched in four digits. "Susie, could you come to my office for a couple of minutes? And bring your records of forty-two's movements."

Three minutes later a pert-looking young woman wearing tight jeans and a light pullover blouse arrived carrying a laptop. "This is Susie Reid, my teaching assistant until we can wrangle another research grant. Susie, this is the Parker family and Casey—"

Susie interrupted, "Casey Carpenter! I'm one of your blog followers."

Casey smiled as they shook hands. "Glad to meet you, Susie. Thank you for your commitment to sustainability."

Katie saw Susie beaming and thought, *Bethany needs to get her act together or she'll lose a good man.*

"Well, good," said Professor Collins. "Susie, the Parkers and Mr. Carpenter are investigating the demise of forty-two. Can you show them her movements?"

"Sure." After opening the laptop and tapping a minute, Susie announced the completed loading of the data by mimicking a whale spotting. "Thar she blows."

The Parkers and Casey gathered behind Susie to see a topographical map with numerous red dots on it. "The tracker recorded her location every hour. You can see how she moved all over, especially in the valleys. But this cluster of dots is on a remote hillside near the park and national forest boundary. Forty-two visited there frequently. She probably died there, because the dots show the collar moving to the dumpster where we found it in Sequim."

Dave spoke for the first time. "So the bear wasn't killed by a car?"

"Definitely not."

"Can you give us a copy of this map, Susie?" asked Katie.

"Do you have an email address?"

"Here's mine," Denyse offered.

After a few taps, Susie brightly announced, "You have it." Then she pointed to her screen. "See the gridlines? They'll give you the approximate GPS location."

The Parkers and Casey thanked Professor Collins and Susie as they prepared to leave.

To Casey, Susie said, "You have my email address In your follower records. Write me if you need anything else."

Back in the rental car, Jeremy asserted, "We need to go see what's at that bear's final location."

Dave answered, "Yes, we do. Your mother and I are good walkers on level ground. But this looks like seven or eight miles each way over rugged terrain and significant rise in elevation. You and Denyse go."

"And me," insisted Casey. "I can bring my GPS."

Denyse looked at her mother-in-law. "Katie, Sandra has been cooped up in the hotel for days . . ."

"Certainly, honey. Dave and I can take care of the children for a day. You should take Sandra and her young legs for a hike in the mountains."

* * *

Aaron stuck his head into the office of DFW's director. "You wanted to see me, Ben?"

"Yeah. Aaron." Director Hodgekiss waved to a chair in front of his desk. "Take a seat."

Aaron sat and waited until his boss spoke again.

"You know that I think you're an excellent detective. DFW is fortunate to have you. And I consider you a personal friend. But lately you've seemed distracted. Is everything okay at home?"

After sighing, Aaron shook his head. "Not really. My family feels like I've abandoned them."

Ben waited while Aaron considered his words.

"I promised Mary to find Hal. I've been turning over every rock and quite a few pebbles. I can't stop searching."

Ben nodded. "I thought so. We all want to find Hal. But all the possible leads have petered out. The state police are baffled. DFW has other cases."

"No case is more important than Hal."

"That's true. But making progress on a secondary case is better than just spinning your wheels. I'm going to give you a few more days, then give you another case. You'll have to let this one go."

Chapter Nine

Denyse, Jeremy, Sandra, and Casey left the rental SUV in a parking area and started on a trail through Olympic National Forest. The trail roughly followed a rushing stream of melted snow under a bright blue sky. "This is wonderful," said Sandra. "The air is unbelievably fresh and clean. It smells like Christmas trees. The forest is like the *Twilight* movies."

"Dave told us that they call Washington 'The Evergreen State' because of these trees," said Denyse.

"We had firs and spruces in Ukraine too. But not so many or so huge. You could make a boat from just one of these trees."

Casey heard Sandra and paused. "Native Americans did make boats, called dugouts, from a single tree. They still do on occasion. Men in several such boats could cooperate to kill a whale and bring it back to their village."

"Is all of Washington like this?" asked Denyse.

"No. Washington east of the Cascade Range of mountains is dryer, even arid. A few parts of the state are considered desert. The huge Columbia River runs from Canada through the arid places and is used for irrigation of crops, especially apples and cherries."

In the valley, their path had passed through boggy areas lush with colorful summer flowers. Reddish-yellow berries lined the trail. "Can we eat the berries?" Denyse called to Casey and Jeremy, who had forged ahead.

"Those are salmonberries," Casey returned. "Help yourself."

Denyse tried one and found it pleasantly sweet and a little tart.

"This is a lot like a raspberry," said Sandra. "We raised many of those in Ukraine. Good for fresh eating. Not so good for pies, unless you mix them with apples."

The trail started to ascend as it traversed the valley's south side. Two-hundred-foot Douglas firs as straight as arrows towered above them. Young trees starting wherever sunlight penetrated the canopy reminded Denyse of Christmas. A tiny squirrel with gray-black fur on its back and a creamy orange underside watched them pass, seemingly unafraid. Its tail formed a question mark. "What is this cute little animal?" Sandra shouted to the men.

"That's a Douglas squirrel," returned Casey. "Douglas is a feisty little creature. I've seen them chasing gray squirrels three times their size."

Denyse had noticed Sandra glancing frequently at clean-cut, handsome Jeremy and recognized what was probably a crush. Dorothy, the accounting firm's secretary, had told Denyse about seductive Giselle's move on Jeremy three years earlier in Mobile and Jeremy's honorable obliviousness. *Sandra admiring a good man is probably a healthy thing for her,* thought Denyse. *Knowing Jeremy could motivate her to make something of herself and to hold out for a decent man.*

"Do you have a boyfriend yet in Australia?" Denyse asked.

Sandra's voice expressed regret. "No . . . I know that I'm not pretty like Sveta, Lena . . . or you."

"Pretty isn't the most important quality to the best men," Denyse returned. "You saw how Sveta had men flocking around her. But they weren't honorable or decent."

"Sveta still has men flocking around her. She's just more discerning than she used to be. And she has a boyfriend that even Lena approves of. But no men are interested in a girl like me."

Denyse decided to try a different angle to encourage Sandra. "What about Bethany?"

"What, what about Bethany?"

"She isn't very pretty. But Casey, who is attractive, adores her. And it's more than a crush. He wants to marry her."

"You are kidding!"

"Open your eyes, honey. Casey loves Bethany. More importantly, he admires and respects her. Watch him to see how a decent man in love acts."

"I can see that in Jeremy around you."

"That's true."

"Do you think Bethany will marry Casey?"

"She will if she's as smart as she seems. Sandra, look for a young man who wants to be your friend. A true friend puts your best interests above his own."

* * *

Jeremy could feel the strain in his legs during the brisk three-hour hike over a rough ascending trail. Snow-covered mountaintops seemed at eye level when glimpsed through Douglas firs. His lungs labored to get enough oxygen at elevations unfamiliar to him. Casey, forty yards ahead, widened the gap between them. Jeremy looked back to where Denyse and Sandra had not yet come into view after the last switchback. "Hold up, Casey!" he shouted. "Let's wait for Denyse and Sandra."

Casey stopped, turned, held a thumb up, and examined his GPS. "We're close," he called back.

Jeremy leaned over with his hands on his knees, gasping to catch his breath. After a minute, his breathing started to slow. He walked to join Casey.

Casey pointed to the hillside between the trail and snow-melt stream. "The topographical map shows bear forty-two frequently visited somewhere down there." He looked at Jeremy. "You kept up well for somebody new to these mountains."

"I guess fishing on my dad's boat doesn't build up much endurance."

"Ah, give it a month and you'd be sprinting over these hills." Casey gestured back down the trail. "There they are." Denyse and Sandra had trudged into view a hundred yards back with their faces down.

Casey pulled water bottles out of his knapsack. "We all need to stay hydrated, even if you don't feel thirsty."

Jeremy sipped the bottle Casey handed him. "How big an area is 'somewhere down there'?"

"Probably within a hundred-yard circle."

Denyse and Sandra slowly approached the men, both breathing heavily. "Need I remind you two that Sandra and I both live near sea level? And that I'm the mother of two children?" complained Denyse.

Casey handed each woman a bottle of water. "You both did fine. Now we're there."

Denyse took a few swallows then surveyed the mountains and recuperated with her hands on her hips. "This is spectacular. Worth the hike."

Casey nodded. "John Muir said, 'Everybody needs beauty as well as bread, places to play in and pray in, where nature may heal and give strength to body and soul.'"

"Why do you suppose that is?" asked Sandra.

"I pondered the power of wild and untamed places like this during our hike in," started Jeremy.

"The grandeur of our surroundings stilled me. I think we humans are filled with petty concerns and our own self-importance. Perhaps the indifference of the mountains, forests, and rivers to us is a reminder of how insignificant we really are. Wilderness gives us a break from ourselves."

The others stared at Jeremy in wonder until Denyse teased him, "From my philosophical and silver-tongued husband. The same one who wanted to interview Sasquatch."

They all laughed, Jeremy the hardest. "Don't you feel it?" he asked.

"I always do," said Casey. "Mind if I use your thought in my blog?"

"Sure. Go ahead."

Casey pointed into the valley. "Let's form a line about twenty-five feet apart and traverse the area. Be careful of your footing off the trail. Call everybody if you spot anything unusual."

"You and Jeremy start first," Denyse said as she chugged more water. "Sandra and I will join you in a few minutes."

Denyse and Sandra joined the line on the second traverse. Denyse was the first to call out. "What happened to this tree?"

The others converged on her to see a young fir with shredded bark up to about eight feet. "That's where a bear clawed and maybe scratched its back," Casey explained. Black hairs remaining in crevices proved him right. He smiled. "This confirms that we're in the right area."

Jeremy grinned. "Maybe a bear is somewhere about."

Denyse gave him a stern look. "Not funny."

On the sixth traverse, Sandra called, "I see something looking like dog food pellets."

Everybody joined her in an open space. Casey's voice revealed excitement. "That *is* dog food. This is a bait station. I can even smell honey."

"Bears eat dog food?" questioned Denyse.

Jeremy answered, "Sure. Bears and dogs are related on the evolutionary tree. And bears can smell twenty times better than a dog. The honey odor could bring them from miles away."

Casey scouted the ground nearby. "Here's a blood spot and some black hairs. Somebody killed a bear right here, probably forty-two. Private hunters baiting bears is illegal. Even feeding bears is illegal. Bears that start associating humans with food are a problem. Only DFW officers can use bait in an official capacity to remove a dangerous bear. DFW uses feed barrels. The blood spot looks relatively recent too. Forty-two's death was illegal poaching out of season. The poachers emptied the food on the ground because a barrel could have been noticed by hikers."

Denyse looked at the black blood spot with horror. "Why would somebody do this?"

"Could be lots of reasons. Maybe a rich client wanted to bag a bear. Maybe someone wanted the skin to sell. And there's always a market for bear gallbladders."

"Why would anyone want the gallbladder?" asked Jeremy.

"A frozen bear gallbladder can bring ten thousand dollars in parts of Asia," answered Casey. "It's an essential ingredient in some traditional medicines. Dried gallbladders are also rather valuable. Let's scout around to see if we find anything else."

A few minutes later, Jeremy shouted, "I've found some bones and a bigger blood spot."

"This was a bear, alright." Casey pointed to the larger blood spot. "See, they skinned it and took the paws. Certainly the gallbladder too. Scavengers stripped the carcass. This is a bear kill zone. Bears will keep coming until gradually all in the vicinity are killed."

Jeremy took photos of the spot.

Denyse looked stricken and sat down on a boulder. "This is a shame."

"And a crime," Casey added. He looked at the sun. "We've found what we came looking for and have a long hike back. Downhill should be quicker and easier than coming up. Let's be extra careful going downhill to not turn an ankle on a loose stone."

* * *

After the hikers returned to Bremerton and reported the bear bait site to the senior Parkers, Katie shook her head in dismay. "Why would people kill bears out of season?"

Jeremy repeated the reasons Casey gave and added, "I've personally seen outrageous prices for bearskins in gift stores."

"I've read about black markets for live animals, especially cubs. Same for cougars, wolves, raccoons, even bald eagles," said Dave.

"Confining any wild animal is also illegal in Washington, except with a special permit," Casey explained.

"So what are we going to do?" asked Katie.

"Obviously, we need to find out who is doing this," said Denyse.

"Why don't we just report this to US Forest Service and National Park Service authorities?" asked Dave.

"I'd like to be able to give them something more," answered Katie. "And, although unlikely, we don't know for certain that some authorities aren't collaborating with poachers."

"We could stake out this spot to see who comes to replenish the bait," suggested Denyse.

"That could be dangerous," Casey warned. "The poachers might weigh your life lightly compared to a prison sentence for themselves. They would also be armed."

"We'd only take pictures," said Denyse. "Jeremy's camera has a telephoto lens that can zoom close."

"How would we put a name with a photo?" asked Katie.

The group remained silent pondering that difficulty until Dave spoke. "We would need a simultaneous parking lot stakeout. Get their license tag number. Bethany could put a face with a license tag. We would need two people at the bait site and two in the parking lot. As pairs, one could watch while the other sleeps."

Denyse looked at Dave with gratitude.

Casey grimaced with regret. "I have speaking commitments and meetings all next week. Everette, Vancouver, Spokane . . . a few other places. I bunched them on my schedule so I could afford renting a car. Influential people are expecting me." He then looked embarrassed. "And donors."

"Jeremy and I can stake out the bait site," offered Denyse. "Camping will be fun." She then looked hopefully at Dave and Katie.

Katie sighed. "Dave and I could watch the parking lot."

"I'll provide some camping stuff for you," Casey promised.

"We need to tell Bethany about this. She found the lead to bear forty-two," said Jeremy.

They all looked at Casey, who appeared sad but didn't volunteer.

"I'll call Bethany," Denyse offered.

Chapter Ten

"So that's what we've planned," Denyse told Bethany over the phone after describing the developments.

"Wow. You've done remarkably. I certainly should be able to identify anybody with a photo and license tag number," said Bethany. "This could be a ring of poachers."

"Casey thinks so too." Denyse paused. "Could I ask how you and Casey are doing? I mean as a couple. He seems crestfallen whenever we mention you."

Bethany's sigh could be heard over the phone. "I like Casey. He's fun and we share common values. But he doesn't have much personal ambition, no decent job or even a car. I've wondered if we married, would I need to support him? I'm just an assistant in the DA's office. I can't see any future in a life with Casey. I'm trying to be honest, like Tara was with Jeremy."

"I just thought I'd ask. How's the sentencing going from the trial you won?"

"Tedious. Getting a conviction is just the first step. The victim impact statements are taking forever. Now lawyers for Stegall are already filing appeals based on technicalities."

* * *

Denise felt bleary-eyed while sitting outside the tent and sipping morning coffee Jeremy had made on a tiny propane burner. "Wilderness is wonderful to walk through and view. Three nights living in it can be less than wonderful. I miss our kids too. When you talked about wilderness giving you a break from yourself, I didn't envision a vacation like this."

Jeremy poured coffee for himself, then started heating water for a dehydrated food packet. "A campfire would make this a lot nicer. I was cold last night."

Denyse nodded. "Yeah, it would. But a fire would be a certain tipoff to those we hope to surveil. And we certainly wouldn't have seen that bear and her cub yesterday because of the smoke odor. I just wish that I had made you carry an air mattress."

"Blowing it up in this thin air would have been interesting." Jeremy smiled. "I heard a noise while you were sleeping last night and turned on my flashlight for an instant. Two bright yellow eyes gleamed back at me. Then the intruder scampered off. Probably a raccoon."

"Maybe a big mosquito," Denyse quipped. "What are they doing in the mountains?"

Jeremy shrugged. "I never thought I'd find more aggressive mosquitos here than on a bayou."

"Poachers wouldn't shoot a mother bear, would they?"

"Apparently they have already. They might also want her cub."

Denyse pulled out a pack of cards to continue a game of gin they had begun their first day camping. "I'm ahead a hundred and eighty-nine to a hundred and sixty-seven. I wonder how your parents are doing."

Katie heard Dave stirring in the rental SUV's back seat at daybreak. "Wake up, sleepyhead. Another fun-filled day in this parking lot."

Dave scrambled forward to take the front passenger seat. "I'm glad July nights are short, being so far north. Is there any hot tea left?"

"No, I emptied the thermos staying awake while you slept. I really need to go to the toilet now."

"You and me both. At least we're in this relatively comfortable SUV. The parking lot even has a port-a-potty. Think about Jeremy and Denyse up there on a mountainside."

Katie started to get out then heard Dave say, "Wait! Somebody is pulling in."

A massive new-looking black pickup truck rumbled up and parked in a space opposite them. A slight man of about thirty-five dressed in camouflage clothes got out of the driver's side. A giant of a man slightly younger and also wearing camo exited the passenger door. In a businesslike manner, they pulled two bulging packs from the truck's open bed. The smaller man helped his companion shoulder the larger pack then put the smaller pack on himself. He looked around then reached into the truck's cab to pull out an automatic handgun, which he put into his jacket pocket.

"They don't look like typical tourists or hikers," Katie whispered. She heard clicks as Dave took pictures through the windshield. "Make sure you get their license tag."

The slight man locked the pickup and started on the trail, followed by the giant. "Why don't you text Denyse? Tell her that two candidates could be headed their way," suggested Dave.

Katie pulled out her phone. "Thank God for satellite links."

"After we've taken turns going to the toilet, I really need a hot tea."

* * *

Jeremy heard Denyse's phone ping. "That's probably Mom."

Denyse read the text aloud. "Two suspicious-looking men—one small, the other large—wearing camouflage clothes are headed your way. They are armed." She looked at Jeremy. "This isn't as much fun as dramas on TV appear. What if they spot us?"

"We've got a good vantage location on the opposite side of the valley. These fir trees hide us. There's no reason they would come over here."

"Are you sure?"

"No. But if we see them headed our way, we'll hightail it over the ridge behind us. If they're the ones, we should spot them in about three hours. My turn to deal the cards."

Nearly three hours later, Denyse whispered, "Two men carrying packs are coming."

Jeremy and Denyse watched breathlessly as the two men left the trail. Carrying the heavy packs, the men cautiously descended the hillside and stopped at the spot where Sandra had found the dog food. Jeremy snapped close-up pictures as the men emptied dog food from their packs. The smaller man opened a jar of honey and poured it onto the pile.

The larger man's voice carried to Jeremy and Denyse. "That should keep 'em coming."

"Always does," the smaller man replied. "We'll have bears when we need them. Let's not hang around, though." The men climbed up to the trail and started back toward the parking lot.

Once the men disappeared from sight, Denyse punched at her phone. "I told Katie that we took pictures of two men emptying dog food on the ground at the bait site."

Denyse read the message that came back. "Good work. Dave says to give them a one-hour head start before you come slowly yourselves. If you happen to run into them on the trail, act like tourists. They won't know anything different." Denyse trembled with relief. "I'm glad that's over."

"Staying up here or getting the photos?"

"Both."

* * *

Two and a half hours later, the men returned to the parking lot with empty packs. Dave photographed them putting the packs into the black pickup and got one more picture of the license tag as they departed. "That had to be the poachers."

"We can compare our photos to the ones Jeremy took to be certain," returned Katie.

"Jeremy and Denyse should be back here in an hour or a little more. Let's stop and get them some hot food on our way back to Bremerton."

"I could use a warm meal myself."

* * *

Two days later the Parkers gathered in Dave and Katie's hotel room while Sandra watched the children next door. Bethany and Casey each attended by Zoom on Denyse's laptop.

"Pictures taken in the parking lot and those of the men planting dog food as bait definitely match," Bethany reported. "Using the license plate number, I found that the owner of the pickup is Willis Boone. He had his last name legally changed from

Rosecrans, maybe to evoke a pioneer connotation. The photo on Boone's driver's license confirms he is the smaller of the two men photographed.

"Records prove that Boone has been ticketed on three prior poaching violations and paid fines. Boone is on a federal watch list for being a member of an extreme right-wing militia group. They call themselves Pioneer Spirit." Bethany paused before continuing. "This militia is steeped in anti-government conspiracy theories and claims the US government is run by liberal tree-huggers. They believe they have a God-given and constitutional right to do whatever they want on government lands. I'm going to put up a picture of the militia's shoulder patch, which clearly shows up in the pictures you took."

A patch with a rugged pioneer holding a muzzleloading rifle with a pistol and a bowie knife in his belt appeared on Denyse's split screen. The pioneer overlaid a fainter image of an AR-15 rifle. Denyse immediately took a screen shot of the image.

Bethany concluded, "Willis Boone owns Pioneer Gun Shop in Shelton. It's frequented by militia members, especially those on the west side of Puget Sound."

The Parkers and Casey contemplated that quietly for a few moments until Katie spoke. "Isn't showing a pioneer from the 1800s on the militia's patch incongruous with a modern automatic rifle?"

Bethany nodded. "Militia groups are always heavy into armament. Makes them feel powerful, I guess. A supposed cause of freedom in their minds is justification to buy guns they want anyway. Gun shows are like a convention to these guys." Bethany paused. "Okay, I exaggerated. Antique gun collectors also frequent gun shows. But militia members do network there."

Dave cleared his throat then read. "In 2016, a group of heavily armed extremists took over the Malheur National Wildlife Refuge in Oregon. Their leader claimed to have received a divine message to do so. Presumably they felt like the wildlife could be used any way they wanted."

"Most in the Pioneer Spirit Militia feel entitled to act with impunity on federal and state lands, and reservations too," added Casey. "Some militiamen are jealous of American Indian lands and express grievances against them. Many militiamen are outraged by having to pay taxes."

"Okay then, subpoena the militia's financial records and I'll take a look," suggested Dave.

Bethany shook her head. "All the evidence we really have right now is some men feeding wildlife. Although the National Park Service warns tourists against that, they don't arrest them. That's not enough for a judge to issue a subpoena. And the probability is that their transactions are in cash anyway."

Dave persisted. "There are law-and-order judges who'll issue a warrant on something as dubious as an anonymous tip."

Bethany nodded. "Yes. But do you want what you find to be thrown out by a higher court? It's moot anyway until we find out who might have the records."

"We need to keep digging. I suggest we find out more about these two men," Katie suggested.

Bethany looked uncertain. "I wouldn't suggest snooping around any of their homes or businesses."

"How, then?" asked Jeremy.

"Let me think," said Katie. "We can figure out a sneakier approach. Maybe we can go in through the front door rather than the back door."

Chapter Eleven

Dave and Katie found the black pickup truck they had photographed parked in front of a rundown building on a back street in Shelton. A sign identified the business as PIONEER GUN SHOP. A neon OPEN sign glowed red in a window. A bell rang as they entered the front door. The Parkers saw Boone—a thin and wiry man with short, unkempt dark hair and scruffy chin bristles. He leaned over a glass counter containing modern pistols in front of a display of mostly semi-automatic rifles. Boone wore non-camo clothes and had a cigarette in his mouth.

Taxidermized animals decorated the shop's walls. In a corner of the shop, a waist-high half-wall marked a workshop. A larger man, tall and muscular with oily-looking blondish hair worn in a ponytail, sat polishing various firearms. His camo clothes displayed the Pioneer Spirit patch. "That's the other man we photographed," Katie whispered.

Katie and Dave started to peruse the aisles of merchandise. There they saw ammunition, survivalist supplies, human-shaped targets, hand-to-hand fighting weapons, and animal traps. Anti-government literature and magazines featuring off-grid living filled a display.

Dave approached Boone. "Nice shop you have here." After receiving a nod and a grunt, Dave continued, "You've got some great game out West. Back in Alabama we harvest a lot of deer, but they're relatively small."

Boone nodded. "Your puny whitetails can't compare with our blacktails or elk."

"Yeah, but on the plus side our state government isn't filled with deep-state tree-hugging liberals."

"You're lucky."

Dave stuck his hand out. "I'm Dave."

Boone shook Dave's hand without enthusiasm and grunted, "Boone here."

Dave then proceeded to brag about hunting and fishing in Alabama. Then he explained, "I've got this remote hunting cabin. I'd like to have something different to impress business clients I take there."

"You ought to try some *big* game hunting out here," said Boone. "Take home a trophy."

Dave lowered his voice. "What I'd really like is a large bear. They're protected in Alabama and small compared to yours on the Pacific Coast."

Boone gestured toward the big man. "Buddy and me offer a big-game guide service."

Dave grimaced. "Too bad this isn't hunting season."

"That don't matter too much if you're willing to pay for a trophy. Three thousand five hundred dollars for a black bear. Six thousand if we can get a rare cinnamon bear. We'll skin it for you and pack out the pelt. We keep the gallbladder."

Dave leaned forward. "We've only got a couple of weeks here. I want to catch a king salmon first. I'll probably be back later. Do you have a phone number?" With the phone number, Dave headed for the door, followed by Katie.

Before they left, Katie recorded the license plate of the only other vehicle, an older-model white pickup, parked in front of the gun shop. "Bethany should be able to find the full name of Boone's accomplice, Buddy."

* * *

Denyse and Jeremy drove a second rented car up the western side of the Hood Canal on Highway 101 eleven miles north of Shelton. "I've never gone undercover before," said Denyse. "You did when helping my brother Trevor in New Zealand. So you do this. I'll just watch."

"Weren't you undercover when we photographed the poachers at the bait site?"

"I meant acting like you're somebody else."

"I'm a little nervous too," Jeremy acknowledged. "The only time I ever did it—that was in New Zealand—Mom and Dad stayed nearby to back me up."

Denyse held up her phone. "The directions say Boone's address is four hundred feet ahead on the left."

"You are at your destination," the phone announced as they arrived at an unpaved driveway.

Seventy-five yards through forest brought them to a decrepit single-story log cabin. Three large mixed-breed dogs surrounded the car barking. A rough-looking woman wearing a sidearm came out the front door. Jeremy lowered the driver's side car window and asked, "Is this the way to Olympic National Park?"

"Only if you're prepared to hike near thirty miles through the national forest. This ain't a parking area. But I'd let you leave your vehicle here all day for twenty bucks."

Denyse observed live traps holding Douglas squirrels and one young raccoon on the cabin's porch. "Can I get out and look at the animals?" she called through her open window.

"Let me tie up the dogs first."

After the dogs had been restrained, Denyse opened the passenger-side door and approached the traps. "Where did you get these?"

"I caught 'em in the woods using apples as bait. I'd sell the squirrels for fifty each, the coon for one-fifty cash. They make special pets," the woman claimed. "Some folks even like to keep a sorta personal zoo."

Denyse's heart broke for the frightened and underfed little animals. "We don't have any cash right now. But how would I transport them anyway?"

"I could let you have a cardboard box. Better if you came back with the cash and some cat carriers."

Denyse looked at Jeremy, who had joined her on the porch. "Okay, we'll come back."

Back in the car and driving down the driveway, Jeremy said, "That was great acting for somebody nervous about going undercover."

"I wasn't acting."

"You don't plan to give her three-hundred dollars for those little animals do you? That'll just encourage her to trap more."

"Yes, I do. These animals need rescuing."

"Are you and I going to get into a fight?"

Denyse smiled at her husband. "Not if you don't fight back."

* * *

Katie greeted Bethany and Casey with hugs that evening when they arrived at the Baymont via the Bremerton car ferry. "We've got a lot to discuss."

"I've already checked the license tag you sent. The second man is Brian Manning, nicknamed Buddy," reported Bethany. "He lives about two miles away from Boone."

Dave recounted their encounter in the gun shop.

Casey bristled at the bear offer. "Fall bear hunting without using bait is legal in Washington. I don't personally want to shoot a bear, but sportsmen are Washington citizens the same as me. The Department of Fish and Wildlife monitors hunting to ensure its sustainability and prevent bears from becoming endangered. Legitimate hunters usually try for the alpha male. When he's removed, a younger bear moves into that territory and is less likely to range out and run afoul of humans. The license fees hunters pay have helped restore wildlife to many areas. But illegal out-of-season hunting with bait could decimate any species' viability."

"What's a cinnamon bear?" asked Denyse.

"That's a black bear by species but light brown in color. Kind of like a naturally blond human," answered Katie.

"The money earned for guiding a bear hunt and selling the bear's gallbladder would explain why off-season bear poaching would be rather lucrative," Dave concluded. "Money is nearly always the major factor. We've uncovered a criminal enterprise here."

"How would they sell the gallbladder?" asked Jeremy. "The woman we met and men we saw wouldn't likely have international connections."

"There's probably a middleman," Katie suggested. As the group pondered that, she nodded toward Jeremy and Denise and asked, "What did you find?"

"Well," Jeremy started, "Boone certainly isn't rich." He described the isolated homestead. "A fraction of the money he quoted Dad would be enticing."

"We saw wild animals in cages at Boone's house," Denyse added. "Some traps had the type of cute little squirrels we saw when we went to find the bear-baiting site."

"Douglas squirrels," Jeremy reminded his wife.

"Right. One trap had a little furry animal with stripes and a mask. Jeremy told me that was a baby raccoon. We don't have those in Australia." Denyse paused. "A woman said she had caught them in the woods. Who would buy wild animals?"

Casey trembled with anger. "Private collections and animal cafés. Raccoons especially are exotic animals around the world. They live their lives in a glass enclosure like a fish tank as decorations."

"Why not a wire cage?"

"To avoid odors. Same with Douglas squirrels."

Bethany gently patted Casey's shoulder. "We're going to do something about this," she promised him.

After calming, Casey explained, "Trapped wild animals probably indicates wildlife trafficking, which is the fourth largest criminal enterprise in the world. Douglas squirrels native to Washington are in great demand as cage pets around the world and a few places in the US. Baby raccoons are irresistible on the exotic pet market. But they grow up into an animal that hates being caged and can do great damage if allowed to run free. All wild animals belong in nature. Unfortunately, wild animals can be sold for good prices."

Casey continued slowly in order to maintain self-control. "If they are selling squirrels and raccoons, they are probably selling other species, maybe little bears or cougars. Those animals would bring thousands of dollars."

The group remained silent for a full minute until Dave spoke. "Katie suggested the possibility of a middleman earlier. That would seem more likely as we discover additional abuses. Without somebody to distribute the animals or animal parts, the locals wouldn't get paid except for when doing business with occasional walk-ins like me. What we need to do is locate the middleman or middlemen."

Nobody had any immediate suggestions of how to do so.

"Bethany, the Washington Department of Fish and Wildlife has jurisdiction here, is that right?" Katie asked.

"That is correct. But they might rush in and only make a few low-level busts. That would alert the middlemen most responsible. And I wouldn't expect any of these militia guys to give up those marketing the animals to avoid a fine or a few months of incarceration. I don't know whether we should involve higher authorities or not. And if we did, who would initially communicate with them? DFW would expect a query from the DA's office to come through proper channels. If I tried, I could be in trouble, maybe lose my job, for running an unauthorized investigation."

Everybody looked at Dave and Katie. "We need to go to the authorities now. But let's first contact them through some respected law enforcement officers," said Dave.

Casey spoke for the group. "How are we going to do that?"

Chapter Twelve

"Is this Director Hodgekiss of the Washington Department of Fish and Wildlife?"

"Yes. To whom am I speaking?"

"I'm Agent Mark Whitten in the Montgomery office of the FBI. We have informants that have information pertinent to you. But these aren't ordinary informants." The agent told a little bit about Dave and Katie's history. "They are great collaborators with law enforcement." Agent Whitten offered the attorney general of Minnesota, a police captain in New Zealand, and lastly a sheriff in California as references for Dave and Katie. "Our informants helped each of them break major cases. The Parkers think they're onto something and want to investigate in cooperation with you, or somebody you delegate. I would welcome their help if I were you."

Director Hodgekiss replied, "Is this the same couple who solved an old murder and broke up a criminal enterprise in Minnesota? The same couple who exposed a human trafficking ring in New Zealand? I've heard rumors about them but thought they had been glamorized by the grapevine. Now they're snooping in Washington?"

"No, they weren't snooping. Somebody in Washington requested their help. Here in Alabama they exposed a white supremacy group running a protection racket on African Americans. Check with the other references I'll send to you. Our informants just seem to fall into these situations. I'm not sure whether that makes them lucky or unlucky. They *are* clever and resourceful. I suggest you hear them out."

* * *

Dave and Katie met Director Ben Hodgekiss in his office at the Natural Resources Building in Olympia. As Dave and Katie were taking their seats, they noticed a mid-forties-looking man sitting in a chair to one side. He smiled politely at them but didn't say anything.

Director Hodgekiss began. "The FBI called me on your behalf. You've been highly recommended as a law enforcement adjunct. Apparently, you cooperated with authorities to break some amazing cases then took a low profile afterwards."

Dave nodded and glanced at Katie. "Katie and I have experienced some . . . challenges."

The DFW director continued, "As a forensic accountant, Mr. Parker, you have also helped governmental authorities get convictions in some difficult cases, including recently in Seattle. Would you now tell us what you've found in Washington?"

Dave looked purposefully at Katie. She began, "We think we have evidence of a militia group poaching and trafficking wildlife."

The director unconsciously leaned back in surprise. "DFW has jurisdiction over all of Washington except for Indian lands and inside the national parks. So, please elaborate."

Katie, with occasional prompting from Dave, described their findings and encounter with Boone. She concluded, "Our theory is that they leave food for the bears on a regular basis but wait for an unscrupulous trophy collector or a buyer before they collect one. Other than guiding illegal hunting, we don't think Boone and Manning have the acumen to sell the poached wildlife themselves. We suspect there is a middleman, perhaps a mastermind."

Director Hodgekiss then gestured at the man sitting off to the side. "Aaron Wierzbowski is a detective in DFW's Special Investigative Unit and an officer of the law in Washington. He is stalled on another case, so I've asked him to determine what you can offer." Dave and Katie examined the thin and well-muscled man, like a college wrestler, with a weathered complexion from a lot of time outdoors.

Aaron spoke for the first time. "You're probably right that Boone and Manning are poachers and that they, and likely others, use a go-between to sell their illicit catches. But how could we find that middleman? I doubt Boone or Manning, being part of an anti-government militia, would give him up."

Dave looked stern. "Would you allow us to go undercover? We've already contacted them. Boone offered us a cinnamon bear. Our Southern accents give us out-of-towner authenticity."

"Endangering civilians in this manner is against DFW policy. We couldn't—"

"But I make the policy," broke in Director Hodgekiss. "I also deplore poachers. The Pioneer Spirit Militia is a public danger. I've talked to the FBI and others about the Parkers. Aaron, you keep Dave and Katie safe and legal as they follow their leads."

"And please keep our partners safe too," Katie hastily added.

"Of course."

* * *

After thanking Director Hodgekiss and exiting his office, Dave and Katie followed Aaron down the hall to a conference room so that the three of them could discuss details further. Katie could sense Aaron seething. She didn't have to wait long to find out what was on his mind.

"I hate animal trafficking," Aaron began with genuine passion. "Poachers work against everything DFW stands for. They steal from nature and outdoors enthusiasts of every type in Washington."

Dave and Katie looked at each other as Aaron fumed. He continued, "Having something illicit gives some people a thrill. Collectors want something that others can't have so they can boast about it. Illicit trophies can become a status symbol within subcultures. If the Mona Lisa painting were to be stolen, some ass would buy it from the thieves. Scarcity makes something valuable. If unicorns were discovered, we'd have to guard them like the rhinos in Africa killed for their horns. Animal parts like bear gallbladders are considered medicine or an aphrodisiac in some cultures.

"Trafficking living wildlife is even worse. DFW found one case of a corrupt vet attaching a port to a live bear to drain fresh gall to sell in Asian markets.

"Sorry for my rant," Aaron apologized after noticing Dave and Katie's expressions of horror. "Let me control myself so we can decide how to proceed."

"No problem, Aaron. We respect your passion and commitment," said Dave. "However, we have thought this carefully through. We want to find the middleman, maybe even his contacts. Can we share an idea with you?"

"By all means do."

"Katie," Dave prompted.

She began, "First, all we can prove so far is that Boone and Buddy are feeding bears. Regarding Boone's offer to guide us on an illegal bear hunt, he could claim that he meant for us to photograph it. You'll need a stronger case to convict him. Because Boone is unlikely to implicate his contacts, even if threatened with prison, we'll need a way, perhaps a ruse, to force him to contact the middleman."

"I'm listening."

Dave explained, "First we'll engage Boone to poach a bear. When he goes through with that, you'll have enough to eventually get a conviction. Also, we'll have gained his confidence so that we can ask for something only the middleman can provide. We would track that exchange."

"Pulling that off will be tricky."

"Yeah, it will. But it's our best shot to convict Boone and discover the middleman. My guess is that Boone isn't the middleman's only supplier."

Aaron ran his hand through close-cropped hair. "You're probably right that there are others. Okay. But I'm going to shadow you all the way. I'll be armed and have technology to contribute."

"Thank you, Aaron," said Katie. Then she asked, "Several other partners are involved in this investigation. Would you be willing to meet with all of us?"

"Sure. When and where?"

"How about tonight about seven at the Baymont in Bremerton?"

"I'll be there."

* * *

The group waited anxiously in the Baymont meeting room for Dave and Katie's return. Once they had arrived, everybody listened attentively as

135

Dave described the meeting at the DFW. "The DFW detective will be here at seven for you all to meet him."

Casey spoke with surprise. "You're going to kill a bear?"

Dave shrugged. "I might have to. The DFW supports our ruse. It should convict Boone and possibly lead to the middleman. We might discover other suppliers and possibly customers."

"Casey, you know this investigation is more important than one bear," said Bethany.

Casey's face showed dismay, but he nodded assent.

Denyse started to object. "I don't see—" She stopped when Jeremy put his hand on her arm.

"That's a long hike in," said Jeremy.

"Your mother and I will manage."

"Mom's going?"

"I'll need her help."

They all heard a knock at the meeting room door. "That should be Aaron," Katie said and opened the door.

Aaron immediately recognized Casey. "Casey Carpenter? I'm Aaron Wierzbowski, one of your blog followers."

"You're a follower?"

"Sure. I'm a hiker and sportsman myself. And DFW is all about sustainability. So this is what your query about unusual findings was about? I sent in a report about mutilated bears."

"Yes, it was. And thanks!"

Then Aaron spoke to Bethany. "Aren't you that wily prosecutor who got the conviction on the fraudster, Anton Stegall? I've seen you on the news. How's the sentencing phase going?"

"Slow. We're still shifting through hundreds of victim impact statements. After the first hundred, they get pretty tedious. Stegall looks like he'd rather be back in his cell. I'm busy getting ready to oppose the appeal Stegall's attorney has already filed claiming judicial bias. They're asking for a new trial. You never know what an appeals court might do."

"But you're also part of this DFW case?"

"Who else traced the license tag leading to Willis Boone? But my role is strictly unofficial."

Aaron shook his head. "I'm not sure the Seattle DA's office would approve of that."

"I'll have to take that chance and hope they don't find out."

"And this is our son, Jeremy, and daughter-in-law, Denyse," said Katie.

Aaron reached out to shake hands with each. "You've been involved with some cases yourselves, I understand."

"Just helping Mom and Dad," said Jeremy. "Denyse and I visited Northwest Trek Wildlife Park. We read that some of their animals came through you. They even have a memorial to a DFW Labrador retriever trained to sniff out illegal wildlife trafficking. I have a lab but he's nowhere near as heroic."

"Ripper saved your skin by sniffing down your mother's cat after you lost him. That's heroic enough," Denyse jibed her husband.

"That's a long inside family story," Katie told the Washingtonians. "Please sit down, Aaron."

"An exciting story, though," Jeremy added.

Aaron smiled and sat down at the table, followed by the others. "I talked to Director Hodgekiss after you left," he told Dave and Katie. "Wearing a wire for your plan is too dangerous. But I'll shadow you close enough to listen and intervene in case of trouble. And I'll give you a GPS tracking device so that I'll know exactly where you are at all times. I'll be armed if you need any help."

Dave nodded. "Thank you, Aaron."

"About this tracking device," asked Katie, "will we wear it around our necks like a bear?"

Everybody laughed.

"No, we'll give the tracker to you to put in your pocket. But I want to warn you that the Pioneer Spirit Militia group could be dangerous. We have a missing agent, Hal Dulfer, who was patrolling in the general area. His car vanished too."

"Is that the case you were stalled on?" asked Dave.

"Regrettably so."

Chapter Thirteen

Denyse heard Bethany clear her throat before speaking.

"I would be surprised if Pioneer Spirit and other militia members aren't involved in all sorts of criminal activity. They play a game of make-believe for adults. If there's no threat, they'll create one in their own heads. In this case, the threat is the government, which prevents them from ravaging the natural resources that belong to all Americans. Being against something gives losers a sense of worth. The bigger the opponent, the more noble they feel. Nothing is bigger than our government. Conspiracy theories traded as fact validate what they want to believe. They say they want the government to return the land to the people. But by 'the people' they don't mean everyone. They mean themselves." Bethany stopped speaking but remained visibly agitated.

Nobody knew what to say after Bethany's tirade. "Anyway, I appreciate Aaron's precautions," Bethany concluded.

Casey spoke up in her support. "I think Bethany is right."

"Then I'll need to quit the Alabama militia," said Jeremy.

The Washingtonians sat stunned until Denyse told them, "Jeremy's pulling your leg, Bethany. He's not part of any militia." His silly grin proved her case. Then Denyse looked at Bethany. "I, we all, agree with you."

* * *

Dave parked the rental SUV in the parking lot of Boone's gun shop. After getting out, Dave and Katie saw Brian Manning, or "Buddy," outside digging a ditch with a shovel. "What's the ditch for?" asked Dave.

"Drainage. We get a lot of rain in wintertime."

"You've got a nice day for it," said ever-friendly Katie.

Buddy squinted up at the sun hanging in a clear blue sky. "Uh-huh."

"Is Willis inside?"

"Yep."

Inside the shop, the Parkers approached Boone, who was leaning over the counter. "Remember me? I was in here a few days ago interested in something special for my hunting cabin in Alabama."

"Oh, yeah."

Dave lowered his voice even though the shop was empty. "Everybody in Alabama has mounted deer and boar heads. I want to make an impression on my clients. A cinnamon bear from Washington was six thousand dollars, right? That will be something nobody else has. I'll contact my bank to wire the money."

"I can't guarantee you a cinnamon. You'll have to take what we find."

"Even a big black bear would be special in Alabama."

"If there are any cubs, they would belong to me," said Boone.

"Okay."

"Could I buy a live bear cub?" asked Katie. "My daughter always wanted one."

"Sure, if we get one. Bring five thousand extra to pay in cash. Meet me at noon day after tomorrow." He described the location of the parking lot they had staked out. "Be prepared to stay a while, maybe overnight."

* * *

Jeremy and Denyse drove up the driveway to the cabin where Boone lived. They had brought with them two cat carriers. The same dogs and armed woman came out. The woman looked at them and started tying up the dogs. After she had secured the dogs, Jeremy and Denyse got out.

"Where are the little animals you had?" asked Denyse.

"They're around back in the shed. We mostly keep 'em out of sight. And the dogs were botherin' 'em."

Denyse and Jeremy followed the woman to a ramshackle shed behind the cabin. Inside smelled of animal urine and decay. Jeremy saw a wire cage with three Douglas squirrels and another with a torpid little raccoon sitting on top of empty larger cages. "What are these cages for?" he asked.

"Sometimes we get bigger animals. Older coons, bobcats, occasionally a fox. My man Boone is hoping to get a bear cub tonight."

"What do you do with them?" "We got an associate who finds good homes for them," the woman snickered. "This is what I have now. Do you want any?"

Jeremy heard Denyse say, "I'll take them all."

"That'll be fifty dollars for each squirrel and a hundred and fifty for the coon."

Jeremy internally grimaced at the cost but respected his wife's compassion. He watched as the woman placed the open ends of their cat carriers and the cages together with practiced ease. She then frightened the little animals to move into the carriers.

While Jeremy counted out three hundred dollars, Denyse asked, "What do you feed them?"

"Use a milk bottle for the baby 'coon. The squirrels will be fine with bread and water."

Leaving in the rental car, Jeremy asked, "Where to now?"

"We went by a Walmart in Shelton. I need to buy a bottle, some cream, and other stuff. Take me there then back to the hotel. I want Katelyn and David to see the raccoon and help me set the squirrels free."

Jeremy nodded. "You got it." After a pause, he said, "We learned something from that woman, didn't we?"

"What's that?"

"They do have an associate. The middleman. He handles larger animals."

"You're right. I was just focusing on these poor creatures."

* * *

Buzz, Buzz. Casey saw Tara Moynihan's name on his phone. "Hello, Tara! How are you?"

"Busy as ever," answered Tara.

Jeff's voice chimed in, revealing them to be on speakerphone. "Who could have imagined that two children could take up so much time?"

Tara spoke again. "Let's switch to Facetime, okay?"

After calling back using Facetime, Casey could see Jeff and Tara smiling at him.

"Ah, that's better," said Tara. "We heard from Dave and Katie that you're working together on a case. How's that going?"

"We're onto a poaching- and animal-trafficking ring involving a right-wing militia group. Pretty serious stuff."

Tara nodded. "I would have expected that with the Parkers."

"But that's not the reason we called," said Jeff. "Tara liked the prospects of the empty department store in that Olympia shopping mall for a new sporting goods store called Outdoors Always. We've signed a lease. We—"

"We want you to manage it for us," Tara broke in.

"But what about my nonprofit, Washington Coalition for Sustainability?"

Jeff spoke again. "That's just the thing, Casey. You can run your advocacy group out of the store. Your facility can serve as the hub of a many-faceted program of outdoors activities and activism. A rallying point for likeminded others. Tara doing that has made our store profitable and resulted in a lot of public awareness for outdoor conservation. Many people are experiencing God's outdoors for the first time."

"You can have meetings at your facility. Offer excursions and classes," Tara added.

Casey felt overwhelmed. "I . . . I . . . don't know."

Jeff came back. "We know you'll need some time to decide. But not too long. The facility lease payments are stretching us. We already have merchandise on order. You'll also need to know our business proposition. Tara?"

Tara started, "You need to remember this is a bit of a shoestring startup. We can cover the lease, arrange a business license, and get inventory on a consignment basis. We'll borrow two hundred fifty thousand dollars using our store in Redwood Hills as collateral for startup costs—"

Jeff broke in. "We're literally betting the store on you, Casey."

Tara smiled and resumed, "Startup costs such as utilities and hiring a couple of outdoors-oriented employees. Your salary target would be eighty thousand a year plus an increasing share of the store's ownership and profits." Tara paused. "But as a shoestring startup, Jeff and I can't possibly afford to pay you from the beginning. Your salary would need to be paid out of sales margins. The success of this venture depends on generating positive margins quickly. I'll come up there for a few weeks to help set up—"

Jeff interrupted again. "Tara is quite a saleswoman."

Tara stared at Jeff, who pantomimed zipping his lips. "To help set up and to model how to serve potential customers. Once the store is profitable, including your salary, all expenses, and the lease payments, we would talk about partnership and profit sharing." Tara looked at Jeff again.

"So, what do you think, Casey?" asked Jeff.

"This is very sudden. I had never dreamed of an opportunity like this. Thank you very much. I'll still need some time to consider your offer."

"Let's say a week," returned Jeff.

"Okay."

*** * ***

At the Baymont, Sandra heard a knock on their hotel room door followed by Denyse's voice. "It's Jeremy and me, Sandra."

Sandra opened the door. Denyse and Jeremy hurried in. She saw an animal carrier in Jeremy's hand and a Walmart bag in Denyse's.

Denyse summoned Katelyn and David from the sitting area at the far end of the room where they were coloring and playing games. "Come see what we've brought to show you," Denyse said.

With Sandra and the children watching, Denyse put on leather gloves and reached into the carrier. She lifted out a timid striped animal and held it securely. "This is a baby raccoon. She's too young to survive in the woods by herself. We're going to take her to a wild animal rescue center in the morning."

As Sandra and the children admired the furry little creature, Jeremy warmed a plastic bottle with a mixture of milk and cream in the room's microwave. He brought the bottle to Denyse. She sat down in a chair then inserted the bottle's nipple into the little animal's mouth. After Denyse squeezed the bottle to force a little fluid out, the little raccoon put its tiny hands on either side of the nipple and forcefully, almost violently, sucked. Everybody heard a trill like a low stuttering murmur come from the baby raccoon.

Katelyn reached out to touch the preoccupied raccoon. "You can touch her. You too, David," said Denyse. "Then Sandra will take you to wash your hands. Wild raccoons can carry diseases."

After they returned from hand-washing, Denyse said, "Hold the bottle, Katelyn."

Katelyn reached out to take the bottle while the raccoon continued to suck. Katelyn turned her head to smile at everyone. "Can we keep her?"

"She's a wild animal and doesn't belong to us, darling. We'll find some people who will help her to grow up before returning her to the woods where she'll be happy."

"Could I feed her too?" asked Sandra.

"Of course, honey." Denyse stood up for Sandra to take her seat and transferred the raccoon to her lap. "Let Sandra take the bottle now," Denyse told Katelyn.

Sandra sat, feeling the baby animal's tugging and manipulation of the nipple. She looked up, beaming. "This is like feeding an orphaned lamb on

Mama and Papa's farm in Ukraine." Tears formed in Sandra's eyes at the poignant memory. "Thank you."

Chapter Fourteen

"Isn't Buddy coming with us?" asked Dave at the trailhead.

"Buddy ain't too bright," answered Boone. "Still lives with his mother. I let him wear the militia patch to make him feel good. He *is* big and strong, though. I keep him around for heavy or tedious work at minimum wage. Plus he can drive his truck whenever I need picked up. I'll call on him to skin your bear and pack the hide out."

This is a long way, thought Katie as she trudged up the trail behind Dave following Boone in the thin mountain air. Dave looked like he was struggling as well. Twice he had asked Boone to slow down and received a response about not bringing a woman next time. *One foot in front of the other,* Katie told herself.

"You two go ahead. I'll collect the rifle. Just stay on the trail," said Boone before he turned into the woods.

As soon as Boone disappeared, Dave pulled out his camera and took a picture of a prominent rock alongside the trail. Dave explained, "Boone probably has that rifle stashed, maybe in a sealed plastic bag. We might need to find it as evidence later."

Katie felt glad for a moment of respite.

Dave smiled at his wife. "You doing okay, sweetheart? This is even tougher than Denyse described."

"Yeah. And she's thirty years younger than we are. Do you want me to carry the pack a while?" Katie asked between gasps for air.

"What would you say if I said yes?"

Katie smiled. "I'd borrow the rifle and shoot you."

Dave chuckled. "That's the spirit." He looked up the trail. "Let's move on but stay at our pace. We're up pretty high. The spot can't be too much farther."

"I wonder where Aaron is?"

"Somewhere close would be my guess."

A half hour later, Boone caught up carrying a vintage, scoped 30-30 Remington bolt-action rifle. "We're almost there. Need to be set before dark," he said then forged ahead. "I'll get everything ready."

Twenty minutes later the Parkers saw Boone waving to them from off the trail. They descended fifty feet to join him on the hillside above a rushing stream. He held up a jar of honey. "This will hurry 'em in."

Dave and Katie watched as Boone scrambled seventy yards into the valley to an open spot. He poured out the honey onto dry dog food then returned to them. "Make yourselves comfortable. We'll be here a while," he said while pulling a huge flashlight out of the pack he carried.

Katie felt relieved to sit down on a rock and catch her breath. She sipped water from a bottle Dave had carried in their backpack. Despite the circumstances, she admired the snow-covered mountain peaks surrounding them. The setting sun cast orangish-pink light on the snowpacks. Dave likewise appeared grateful for the rest.

After a minute of fussing with the rifle, Boone handed it to Dave and pointed. "Look through the scope at that open space." After Dave had done so, Boone continued. "Now lie down on your stomach and rest the barrel on this fallen tree. Can you still see the open space?"

"I can."

"Now we wait. You can lie down too, if you like," Boone said to Katie before putting his back to a tree trunk and covering himself with a light tarp.

Katie lay on her back on Douglas fir needles. The odor of fir trees her buoyed her spirits. She watched the first stars appearing above her steadily multiply until the black sky seemed impossibly crowded. The Milky Way made a broad path from one horizon to the other in the moonless dark. The bright stars alone provided enough light to see shapes and movements. *We can't watch the stars this well in Alabama,* she thought. *Probably because of the natural haze and lights from the city.*

Without the warmth of hiking exertion, the air started feeling chilly. *I'm glad Denyse insisted that I bring this jacket,* Katie thought. Soon the chilly air turned cold. The whine of mosquitos began. *Something else Denyse warned me about.* She imagined Denyse and Jeremy staying on the mountain for three nights while she and Dave had staked out the parking lot. *Denyse is a trouper.*

Several hours seemed to last an eternity. A thin, waning moon had risen, giving more light but diminishing the stars. Katie could see that Dave, uncomfortable on his belly, had rolled onto his side and taken a fetal position against the cold. She heard Boone whisper, "Do you hear that? We got one coming."

Katie could hear something pushing through the undergrowth and the crunch of feet on dried leaves.

Dave rolled back to his stomach and positioned the rifle on the log. Katie rose to a kneeling position in the dark.

Boone's voice revealed excitement as he instructed Dave in a whisper. "You'll see the bear eating in a moment. Don't worry. This old rifle will shoot straight. I've killed plenty of animals with it. Even one two-legged one who tried to deny me my rights. The rifle has been sighted in for this range. Hold steady and you can't miss. Now be ready."

Five seconds later a beam of light pierced the darkness, illuminating a bear eating. Surprisingly, the bear didn't seem to be alerted by the light. Katie saw a small cub sniffing around beside its mother. "Just put the crosshairs behind her front leg and slowly squeeze the trigger," whispered Boone.

Katie saw Dave point the rifle at the bear and take a deep breath. Katie coughed aloud. The bear immediately reacted. Dave fired, a tremendous explosion of sound and flash of light in the quiet night. A puff of dirt revealed the bullet impact on the ground where the bear had been.

Boone cursed as the bear crashed through the undergrowth escaping.

"Why did you make noise?" Dave demanded with anger.

Katie's voice indicated sorrow. "Sorry. It was involuntary. I couldn't help coughing. The night air . . ."

Dave turned to Boone. "The bear moved just as I was pulling the trigger. We'll still pay you."

"Damn right you will."

Katie listened with her head down as Dave and Boone haggled, considering they didn't get either bear or cub. She finally saw Dave count out $6,500 dollars for the lost bear and cub. After giving Boone the money, Dave said, "I've still got my heart set on a trophy for my cabin. But I only have a few days remaining and don't want to go back to Alabama empty-handed. Can I buy something already collected?"

Boone had calmed down after being paid. "I'll have somebody call you in a coupla days." He picked up the rifle.

"Give him our phone number," Dave ordered Katie.

She pulled out a scrap of paper and a stubby pencil, wrote down their number, and handed it to Boone. "Remember that I still want a bear cub."

"You two know the way down," Boone growled. "Just follow the path and wait for a call." The Parkers saw Boone's flashlight bouncing as he returned to the path and started home, leaving them behind.

Dave pulled a small flashlight out of his pack. "Nice plan, sweetheart. You coughed at just the right moment. I really didn't want to kill a bear tonight."

"Me neither. Aaron has our phone monitored. Maybe that will lead us to the middleman. I wonder where Aaron is now."

"Closer than you think," Aaron's voice startled the Parkers. "Nice trick, to save that sow bear."

"Have you been here the whole time?" asked Katie.

Aaron chuckled. "Since dark, anyway."

His response amazed Dave. "How did you do that?"

"Ten years as an Army Ranger." Aaron then looked intently at Dave and Katie. "You two keep your wits about you, don't you?"

Dave reflected the compliment with a quip. "Thanks. But getting into the situations we do makes me think we're both half-wits. Together we probably have a whole wit. One wit isn't as hard to keep."

While smiling, Aaron reached out to give Dave a congratulatory tap on the arm. "If you're willing, let's try walking out slowly and quietly in the natural moonlight. That way, we'll be able see Boone's light before he sees us in case he decides to tarry."

"He'll probably take some time stashing the rifle," said Dave.

"Oh, he leaves the rifle up here somewhere? That makes sense. I wondered about his detour off the trail."

The secure and relatively leisurely walk out without artificial light through the mountains and forest under the night sky delighted Dave and Katie. Aaron even provided snacks and mosquito repellant.

* * *

Early in the morning, Casey picked up a key from the mall office in Olympia and entered the facility Tara and Jeff had leased. The former department store offered twenty-seven thousand square feet of merchandising and activity space. Trusses supported the ceiling twenty-five feet above him. His footsteps echoed loudly in the empty space. He examined pictures Tara had sent from their store in Redwood Hills and visualized departments and displays of bikes, camping gear, clothing, fishing tackle, birding supplies, kayaks, skis, and more. "Plenty of room here," he said aloud.

Behind the bar of a customer service center, he found four administrative offices. A door opened to a conference room that could accommodate a hundred participants. *A wonderful place for meetings,* he realized. *If I took this job, would Bethany think I was selling out my beliefs for money? Maybe not if we make this a center for outdoor activities and sustainability efforts across Washington like Tara suggested. Would managing the store leave enough time to blog about sustainability issues? I could take pressure off of myself by welcoming other outdoors advocates as contributors. Doing so would likely generate regional awareness of the store and serve as low-key marketing. The potential here is unlimited.*

Casey's thoughts turned into daydreams. *I could offer Bethany one of the offices. She could legally represent sustainability issues.* Reality hit him hard. *Bethany is committed to her job in the Seattle legal system. She's good at it and would never give up seeking justice for victims.*

Denyse led Katelyn by the hand as they made their way into the deep forest at Ueland Tree Farm, not far from the Baymont. Sandra walked beside her, holding the carrier with the tiny Douglas squirrels. Jeremy followed, carrying David on his shoulders.

"See them for the last time," Denyse said to the children as they all stood among towering trees.

"Your mother saved these little animals and is giving them a good life," Jeremy added.

David started to insert his finger through a breathing hole. Denyse pulled his hand back. "They don't know that you're their friend. One might bite you." She nodded to Jeremy, who opened the carrier door.

The squirrels didn't dart out to safety as everybody expected. "What's the matter?" asked Sandra.

"They're probably just frightened," said Jeremy. He gently picked up the carrier and tipped it until the three squirrels tumbled out. Each one disappeared into the undergrowth in an instant. "Have a good life, little squirrels."

An hour later, Jeremy and Denyse along with Sandra and the children parked in a graveled lot and exited the rental car. A sign proclaimed OLYMPIC WILDLIFE CENTER: LICENSED WILDLIFE REHABILITATOR. Covered chain-link cages sprawled out behind a small office.

A middle-aged and disheveled woman came out of the office and hurried toward them. "Thank you for calling ahead. My name is Madeline," she said. "I talked to Aaron Wierzbowski, who told me you're cooperating with DFW to rescue some trapped animals."

"I saw online that you accept raccoons," said Denyse. "We have a little female. But aren't you afraid of rabies?"

"Rabies in raccoons is very rare in western Washington. But we *will* isolate her for a few weeks to be certain." The woman looked at the carrier in Jeremy's hand. "Is this her?" After Jeremy handed Madeline the carrier, she held it at eye level, looked through the door, and spoke soothingly. "You're safe here, little one. We'll take care of you."

"Will you release her to the wild once she's grown?" asked Jeremy.

"We'll try. That depends on how accustomed she has become to humans and whether we can teach her to find food in the woods. If we think she'll starve or look for people to feed her, then we'll find someplace for her to have a good life."

"Thank you," said Denyse. "Say goodbye," she told Katelyn and David.

Katelyn started to cry. "I want to keep her."

"We can't, honey. But this lady is an expert and will take good care of her."

"I will," promised Madeline.

Chapter Fifteen

Katie woke late in the afternoon following a wee-hour arrival back at the hotel. The clock said 1:37 p.m. She rolled out of bed and used the room's microwave to make hot water for tea. She saw Dave stir and called, "Wake up, sleepyhead."

Dave forced his feet to the floor then stumbled to the bathroom. Katie heard the shower. *I'll order pizza delivery for lunch,* she thought and picked up the phone.

Gentle rapping on the room's door stopped her. Jeremey's voice came through. "Ya'll up, Mom?"

Instead of answering, Katie opened the door. "Come on in. Your father is waking up in the shower."

"What happened on the bear hunt?" asked Jeremy.

"All went well. But let us tell everybody at once. Could you set up a Zoom call with yourselves, Casey, and Bethany say . . . in an hour?"

"Of course."

An hour later Dave and Katie logged into Zoom. The others waited, Bethany in Seattle and Casey in Olympia. They all laughed and sighed with relief when Katie described their ploy to avoid killing the mother bear. Dave gave the conclusion. "So we're waiting for a phone call from the potential middleman. Boone sounded like that could take several days. Nothing to do until then."

Everybody remained silent until Casey suggested, "Why don't you go on a salmon charter? The king salmon are swarming out of La Push on Washington's coast."

Jeremy visibly brightened at the idea. Denyse said, "I think Katie and I could do something with Sandra and the children. You guys go." Katie nodded consent.

"Casey, you should come with us. You could write a blog about it," invited Dave.

Casey temporized, "Or I could take you clam digging."

Sensing Casey's financial situation, Dave elaborated, "Salmon fishing as my guest."

Casey's face lit up. "Sure! Thank you, Dave."

Bethany proposed, "I'm off work tomorrow. I'll take the rest of us sight-seeing and shopping."

Boone dialed a number and waited impatiently as he listened to the phone ringing. "Hello," a gruff voice answered.

"Captain, this is Willis Boone. I got a deep-South tourist here says he wants somethin' special for a private hunting cabin."

"Has he got money?"

"Yes, sir. He's flush. Gave me sixty-five hundred for a failed bear hunt. Wants a trophy to display. Bear rug or somethin' else. His wife wants a bear cub."

"You good with a thousand for the hand-off?"

"Yes, sir."

"Okay, gimme the tourist's number."

Dave, Jeremy, and Casey had left at 2:00 a.m. for a four-hour drive to the salmon charter. "Why does the Elwha River sound familiar to me?" asked Jeremy while driving on Highway 101 toward La Push.

Casey sat in the passenger seat. "You probably heard about the removal of the hundred-and-five-foot Elwha Dam and hydro plant in 2011. That was the largest dam removal in US history. At the same time, the government also took out the two-hundred-and-ten-foot Glines Canyon Dam upriver. The dams had been built in the early 1900s to power a pulp mill. But they destroyed the ecosystem and infringed on American Indian rights. That was twenty-five years before the land became part of Olympic National Park."

"Why did they remove the dams?"

"To return the Elwha River and ecosystem to their natural state. In particular, the dams had destroyed a vigorous salmon run that supplied food to the Lower Elwha Klallam tribe of Indians, as well as bears, eagles, otters, and other wildlife. I have mixed feelings about the removal," Casey confessed. "The dams produced nearly thirty megawatts of sustainable electric power without burning fossil fuels. But the ecosystem has recovered faster than anyone had imagined. We now have seventy miles of beautiful river to enjoy. And even without those dams, hydro power provides sixty-five percent of electricity in Washington, thirty-one percent of the nation's total."

Dave spoke from the rear seat. "Can you fish in the Elwha?"

"The river has been closed to fishing. But the salmon have returned and are increasing yearly. I think DFW plans a limited opening soon."

Highway 101 narrowed to two-lane traffic and started to wind around pristine Crescent Lake surrounded by evergreen-covered mountains. "This is really gorgeous," commented Jeremy. "Are they going to remove this lake's dam too?"

"This lake was formed by a landslide about eight thousand years ago and is natural."

Jeremy and Casey continued to chat, passing through prehistoric landscapes and across sparkling rivers. After a lull, Casey announced, "I've never been on a fishing charter before. Thank you for bringing me, Dave."

"You're welcome, Casey."

"I've never been on a charter boat before either," said Jeremy. He gestured toward the back seat where Dave stared out the window at a snow-covered mountain peak. "Dad has a boat in Mobile. We're descendants of professional fishermen. Some of my earliest memories are fishing and crabbing on Mobile Bay. No need to charter a boat."

Bethany drove her SUV past a large statue of a Viking then down Front Street in Poulsbo. "A lot of Norwegians immigrated here to fish Washington's waters," she said. In the old shopping district, she pointed to Nordic-themed shops and decorations. "When commercial fishing in Puget Sound declined, the town went tourist."

"This is charming," said Denyse, looking out the window. "Can we stop and look around?"

"Of course." Bethany found a place to park.

Followed by Bethany and Denyse, Katelyn and David raced to nearby playground fixtures on the north side of Liberty Bay under a bright blue sky and crisp-cool July air. Katie pulled Sandra aside and whispered. Bethany saw her slip the young woman a hundred-dollar bill. Sandra hugged her.

Sandra then led everyone to the gift shops, where she carefully scrutinized merchandise. Denyse perused the expensive art galleries but didn't buy anything. Sluys Bakery drew Katie, where she purchased treats for all. When they passed the open door of a historical museum, Denyse wanted to go in. Sandra wistfully looked back at gift shops yet unvisited. "We can split up," Katie suggested. "I'll return to the park with the children."

"I'll help you watch them," Bethany offered and looked at Denyse and Sandra. "Back in about an hour?" Both Denyse and Sandra nodded and hurried away.

Bethany and Katie sat in a shady spot watching the children play in Waterfront Park. "You and Dave have a remarkable relationship. The way you work together amazes me," said Bethany.

Katie smiled. "We grew apart for a while during my mother's lingering illness and while Dave was striving to build his accounting firm. We had stopped communicating unless you count arguments. Jeremy running away from home woke us up."

Bethany's face showed surprise. "Jeremy ran away?"

"Yes. Ten-year-old Jeremy got the idea that he was the cause of Dave and me arguing so frequently and decided his departure could solve our problem. Fortunately, he took our Labrador retriever Ruthie with him. A friend called us the next morning when they arrived at her house. But that showed us how unhappy he was. We immediately made changes, starting with Dave and me cooperating more and having fun as a family."

"Jeremy and Denyse seem to be doing well," said Bethany.

"Yes, they are. Denyse has become the daughter we hoped for. If ever they were to split up, I'm keeping Denyse." Bethany laughed at Katie's joke.

"They occasionally have a tiff over something, though. All functional couples do," Katie continued. "Do your parents live nearby?"

"My parents moved to Arizona three years ago. They had become tired of Seattle's dreary, wet, overcast winters."

The mother instinct in Katie forced her to probe a little. "You and Casey are friends, right?"

"Yeah, Casey is a great guy." Bethany then paused. "I got married in high school at eighteen, Katie. Was divorced at twenty. Henry was the captain of our school's football team when I was a cheerleader. He was such a bruiser everybody called him Hulk. He seemed so heroic fighting for our school's honor on the field. I felt privileged to nurse his hurts and bruises. Universities aggressively recruited him. Everybody expected Hulk to be a shoo-in for the NFL. I could picture myself married to a millionaire football player and sitting in the enclosed luxury skybox seats. Then I became pregnant. His parents made him marry me and my parents agreed. After we married, I lost the baby. Maybe because of inadequate prenatal care. Maybe because Hulk was so rough during my pregnancy." Bethany stopped for moment, then continued with difficulty. "I've never been raped. But I think I know what that must feel like."

Katie reached out and touched Bethany's hand. "I'm so sorry, honey."

Bethany sighed. "Hulk's answer to any problem was anger and aggression. Not all football players are dumb, but he was. They had held him back three different years in school. That also made him older, bigger, and stronger than the other high school players. But it should have tipped me off that Hulk wouldn't always have that advantage. He never made the NFL. Didn't even finish his college eligibility."

"What happened to him?"

"I don't know. I hope he's a garbage collector somewhere."

After Bethany remained silent, Katie asked, "How did you meet Casey?"

"We met on a group backpacking trip organized by his outdoor advocacy group. I think Casey loves me, and he even mentioned marriage recently. I pretended not to hear. He's certainly sweet. But I work long hours. We go to movies, fast food, sometimes hiking. He overnights at my apartment maybe once a week. I've never even seen where he lives. But I'm getting all I need out of our current relationship. No need to change."

Bethany and Katie saw Denyse and Sandra returning together. Sandra carried several bags with purchases. "What have you bought?" asked Bethany.

Sandra gushed, "I've got presents from America for my sisters, Lena and Sveta."

Bethany nodded. "Let's go to Bainbridge Island next. I'll treat everybody to a late lunch."

* * *

Casey watched Jeremy and Dave as the twenty-five-foot fishing boat motored away from ramshackle docks and past towering rock formations scattered along the coast of the Indian reservation of La Push. They seemed relaxed and at ease while leaning on the boat's gunnel and staring at barking sea lions. Casey heard the Indian captain yell, "They'll be waiting for a share of your fish when we return."

Jeremy moved to stand next to their captain and guide so he could ask questions about navigation and fishing. Dave simply sat in the open stern, relaxed, breathing deeply, and surveying the seagulls circling above choppy water. *The Parkers have spent a lot of time on open ocean,* realized Casey.

An hour later and out of sight of the coastline, their guide cut the engine and hurried to the stern, followed by Jeremy. "The fish finder shows the biggest school of fish I've ever seen," said Jeremy.

From plastic pipe holders above the cabin, their guide pulled down three stout rods rigged with baitcast crank reels and round half-pound lead weights. He quickly impaled a six-inch herring into a large barbless hook on a leader below the sinker, swung the rig into the water, handed the rod to Dave, and said, "Lower to ninety feet then slowly raise the bait through the school."

The guide had just swung a rig for Jeremy into the water when Dave's rod tip jerked down and stayed down. Dave raised the rod tip to set the hook and continued holding it high. Casey saw the rod bow downwards and the line slicing through the water.

"Hold up to avoid a tangled line," the guide told Jeremy. He then grabbed a four-foot-wide net on a ten-foot handle from the tubular rod holders above the cabin.

Casey watched Dave position his rod's butt end on his stomach. Dave reeled in line as he lowered the rod tip toward the water. The reel screeched as the fish's pull exceeded the reel's drag setting. Dave raised the rod tip high again then reeled in again as he lowered it. Raising and lowering the rod tip, Dave gradually pumped the fish toward the boat. Its exertions grew less strenuous. After several minutes, Casey saw a long silver fish writhing in crystal clear water ten feet under the boat. Once Dave had raised the fish to the surface, the guide suddenly lunged with the net and pulled a flopping salmon onto the boat.

The guide leaned over the fish for a moment, shook his head, slipped out the barbless hook, then dropped the fish overboard. Dave somehow looked both crestfallen and elated.

"Why didn't you keep it?" asked Jeremy.

"Had an adipose fin. Proves it was a wild salmon spawned in a river. They cut the adipose fin off hatchery fish in Washington. Those we can legally keep up to a limit of two per fisherman. Unless a bear gets him first, that fish will spawn in a river," the guide explained.

Dave shrugged and reached for a herring to rebait as their guide prepared a rig for Casey. Jeremy began lowering his bait. The guide put Casey's rig into the water and returned to the cabin to check the fish finder. Dave noticed Casey looking at the reel and showed him how to rest the rod on the boat's gunnel, release the brake, apply his thumb to control lowering, and use the depth indicator to position his bait at ninety feet. "Gradually reel up and watch the tip. The tip should tell you when a fish takes the bait. After you get a fish on, jerk up to set the hook, then position the rod butt on your stomach."

"Fish on!" called Jeremy.

Casey turned to see Jeremy's rod bending. He watched Jeremy pumping in the fish for a few moments, until he felt Dave pull his sleeve and say, "Look at your rod, son."

Casey turned his head to see his rod tip turned downward and quivering. He lifted the rod tip as he had seen Dave do and immediately felt the fish's strength. He struggled to place the rod's butt into his stomach and heard the reel screech.

Their guide hurried back and attended to Jeremy first. Casey heard Dave instructing him. "Lower the rod tip and reel. Then raise up. Lower, reel, and raise."

Casey felt his arm aching as he fought the fish. Despite himself, Casey looked to watch Jeremy's struggle. Although he had made progress at first, Jeremy could no longer lower and reel. Jeremy's reel screeched continuously.

Inexplicably, the guide left Jeremy and came to Casey. "You're doing fine. Bring him in," said the guide.

In another minute, Casey saw a fish larger than Dave's in the water below. After three more lower and reels, the guide again lunged with the net and brought the fish onboard. After a quick inspection, the guide muttered, "Nice king, 'bout thirty pounds," and produced a club from someplace. He struck the fish's head behind its eye then heaved it into a cooler that also served as a seat in the center of the stern.

Casey turned his attention to where Jeremy and Dave were staring at a point where the line entered the water. Despite pulling, Jeremy could not bring the fish closer. *He must have a whale,* Casey thought. Suddenly something splashed where Jeremy and Dave stared. A harbor seal's head appeared with Jeremy's salmon in its mouth.

Chapter Sixteen

The guide joined them and shook his head. "Just hold on," he said with disgust. "Let me see your salmon card," he told Casey. Casey pulled the card from his pocket and handed it to the guide, who pulled out a pencil and recorded the date, area, and catch.

Casey looked back to Jeremy in time to see the jerking of the rod tip stop. Jeremy steadily reeled in something without pumping. A salmon head attached to the hook appeared.

The guide lifted the line by hand, deftly twisted the hook, and let the head fall into the ocean. Their guide looked at Dave. "If you'll rebait the lines, I'll reposition the boat over the school."

The understated small town of Winslow on Bainbridge Island charmed Katie and the others. The women and children walked down Winslow Way with Denyse holding Katelyn's hand and Sandra pushing David in a stroller. "This is one of my favorite places to eat when I take the ferry over from Seattle," said Bethany as she guided them to a restaurant with outdoor seating under an arbor covered with blooming clematis vines. "You can try seaweed bread, kelp Caesar salad, or Dungeness crab toast if you like. And they have a key lime pie to die for."

Katie noticed that Bethany maneuvered the seating to place herself between the two children. During the meal she chatted with Katelyn, asking her questions about her school. She tickled David and made him smile with funny faces. Suddenly Katelyn pointed and said, "Santa Claus."

Everybody looked to see a portly man with a pure white beard at a nearby table. "Don't point," Denyse told her daughter. "He does look like Santa," Denyse agreed. "Santa look-alikes seem common in western Washington compared to Alabama."

"Really?" asked Bethany. "Since I live here, I don't notice. What else appears unusual to you?"

"Well, we're not used to cannabis stores," answered Katie. "Tattoos and piercings are more common here, and we don't have casinos operated by American Indians."

"I know that our cost of living is high," said Bethany.

Denyse nodded. "From what I've seen, Washington is worth higher costs."

"If you want to see strangeness, come visit us in Cajun country along the Gulf Coast," said Katie. After a pause, she added, "I mean really. We would welcome you to visit . . . and Casey."

The children became restless once they had finished eating. Denyse and Sandra took them for a walk in the direction of a park by Eagle Harbor, leaving Katie and Bethany at the table.

Katie prompted, "Katelyn and David really like you."

Bethany smiled and nodded. "I like them too."

"Would you like to have children of your own someday?" Katie asked.

"Sure. I guess. But I couldn't settle down and be a mother and housewife. I need to accomplish things."

"Do you know that Denyse teaches calculus in an inner-city high school? She helps a lot of teenagers get off to good careers. The district has asked her to oversee improving math standards in all their schools."

"No, I didn't know that. That's so cool!" Bethany's voice communicated genuine respect.

"You said that you were getting all you needed from your relationship with Casey. Maybe you need things you don't realize," Katie suggested. "Are you sure of what you want in life?"

Rather than answer directly, Bethany said, "How could a marriage to Casey work out? He and I are in different places. His nonprofit organization doesn't provide enough for him to even afford a car. Would I have to pay for everything on my salary? I can barely rent an apartment in Seattle, much less buy a house. I need somebody with more personal ambition. At least Hulk wanted to become a pro football player."

"In this case, you and Casey are not fundamentally different. You're both passionate about causes. You commented on my and Dave's relationship and our teamwork. We work well together now because we are different. We learned that differences can make a couple stronger as a team because each contributes different strengths."

Bethany listened intently as Katie continued, "Honey, you may not need more from Casey right now. But as you get older, you'll find a companion—one who truly and unselfishly loves you—makes life much better, even if your relationship has rocky periods." Katie paused before prompting, "Casey seems to be considerate and generous."

"He is that," acknowledged Bethany.

"He's obviously smart and capable too. His blog and the group he leads prove that," Katie continued. "As a bonus, Casey is rather handsome."

Bethany stared at Katie with her mouth agape.

Katie shrugged. "You think because I'm happily married and older that I don't notice?"

* * *

Jeremy looked into the rearview mirror while driving back to Bremerton. He saw Dave asleep in the back seat and behind him a cooler filled with fillets from six king salmon and four large rockfish caught after their salmon limits had been filled. "That was some great fishing," he said to Casey in the passenger seat. "You caught three of our six salmon keepers."

Casey could hardly restrain his excitement. "I'd never caught any salmon. But I've eaten small pieces before. The best of any fish. I'm sorry your father only caught one keeper, though."

"Dad's plenty happy. He caught four wild salmon. One of them nearly thirty pounds. And seeing you catch fish made him even happier than if he had caught them himself."

"You and he have fished a lot together."

"Yes . . . we . . . have." Jeremy continued to tell Casey about sustainable fishing in the Gulf of Mexico, the artificial reefs, freshwater fishing upriver, crabbing, and oystering. "I once saw Dad catch a sailfish while trolling for king mackerel. I wondered how sailfish would taste. Because sailfish have gotten scarce, Dad hardly paused to get a picture before getting it back into the water."

Casey nodded in appreciation. "I wish everybody was as conscientious."

"What did you do before starting a sustainability nonprofit?" asked Jeremy.

Casey sighed. "I grew up in Southern California. My parents ran a 7-Eleven. Los Angeles, Long Beach, Orange County . . . it was all the same. Subdivisions, apartments, dilapidated shopping centers, service stations. Drive a hundred miles in any direction and you're still in town. Although I lived there, it never felt like home. You know what I mean?"

Jeremy nodded, although he hadn't experienced that.

"Anyway," Casey continued, "I joined the Navy to get away. Got assigned to a carrier, the USS *Nimitz*. Worked in the laundry. Six thousand people, mostly men, crammed into a space about the size of three football fields. That didn't feel like home either. I spent most of my free time on computers. Fortunately, the *Nimitz* is based in Bremerton. Five minutes from there and you can be in deep woods or on the sound. I felt the presence of God the first time I hiked in the Olympic Mountains."

"I sometimes feel close to God on Mobile Bay or in the Gulf of Mexico," Jeremy responded. "I think Dad does too."

Casey nodded before continuing, "I used my GI benefits to attend The Evergreen State College in Olympia. Didn't know what else to study, so I became a business major. But I took a few electives related to conservation and sustainability. Afterwards, I managed a Burger King for a couple of years and wandered outdoors during my spare time. Gradually I became convinced that God's outdoor cathedral needed to be preserved. Later I found that a lot of people think the same way. So I quit the burger business and started the nonprofit. As a business major, you'd think I'd have created a business plan first. But I didn't. So I live on twenty-five and fifty-dollar donations through my website. After a couple of years, my old car broke down and I couldn't afford repairs. So now I use public transportation and live in a single rented room with a hotplate."

"How did you meet Bethany?"

"She joined a group backpacking trip I organized for my blog followers. She's two people. As an attorney, she's like a well-dressed shark. As an outdoors enthusiast, she's a totally different person."

"Yeah, we all saw the shark part when she had us sign that non-remuneration contract. A woman like her has a bewitching quality that no matter how well you know her, you never get bored. Denyse's passion for her students to learn mathematics makes her like that too."

Casey laughed. "I can't help but love Bethany. But she lives in a different world than me. Makes a lot of money. Has an apartment in an expensive high-rise in the city. Drives a loaded Lexus. Mixes with important people, like . . ." Casey used his thumb to indicate Dave in the back seat.

That was Jeremy's turn to laugh. "Both Mom and Dad *are* pretty important. But Dad is two people like Bethany. At the accounting firm, he's exacting and professional. But you should see him out in his boat."

"You're right. I saw Dave catching salmon today as happy as any kid." Both Jeremy and Casey laughed.

Jeremy's tone became more personal. "I'm not knowledgeable about relationships like Mom is. But

I do know that every relationship is unique. Your relationship with Bethany is a bit unusual. Commonly, but not aways, the men are less emotional, more driven, and dependent on logic. Women are generally more compassionate, sensitive to others, and more verbal. You and Bethany are somewhat switched.”

“Reasonable. But what should I do?”

“Maybe like Bethany has two sides, you could develop your more professional side.”

“I could have an opportunity to do that and still be an advocate for the outdoors.” Casey told Jeremy about Tara’s offer. “I’ve got a big decision to make.”

“I have a big decision looming myself,” said Jeremy when Casey finished. “People in Alabama are urging me to run for public office this fall.”

“Really? I’d vote for you. If you won, you’d need to develop a political side.”

“That’s what worries me.”

* * *

Alerted by a phone call from Casey, all the women met the returning fishermen in the hotel lobby. Jeremy carried a cooler with seventy pounds of fish fillets. Dave babbled about catching salmon, rockfish, and even one shark. "Jeremy tried to catch a seal," he jibed his son.

"Have *you* ever had anything that big on a line?" Jeremy retorted.

Katie rolled her eyes and muttered where only the women could hear, "Men and fish!" After Denyse snickered, Katie spoke more loudly with emphasis, "Oh, fish! We would have starved without our men."

Everybody laughed. Dave started to temporize, "Actually, at supermarket prices, we brought home more value than the seven hundred fifty dollars we paid for the excursion."

"Then we'll be rich if you go fishing every day," Katie added, bringing more laughter.

"Have you and Jeremy considered how you're going to store your fish and then carry them back to Alabama?" asked Denyse.

Dave's surprised expression revealed that they hadn't.

Katie further elaborated. "I'm sure this hotel wouldn't appreciate guests cooking fish in the microwave."

As Denyse clowned by pinching her nose, Jeremy's happy expression turned to angst.

"I know a lot of people who could never afford to buy salmon. I could distribute this to some who would be really grateful," offered Casey. He looked at Bethany and confessed, "I hardly make minimum wage from my blog and nonprofit. Many of my neighbors are even worse off."

Bethany spoke to the others, "If you're all willing to take Casey's offer, then we'll be off to deliver the fish." After nods all around, she added, "We'd better get going then."

Casey looked surprised. "You're coming along?"

"Aren't we partners?" When Casey remained stupefied, Bethany picked up the heavy cooler and struggled toward her car.

Casey looked at the others, who all gestured for him to go. He hurried to catch up to Bethany and took the cooler to carry.

* * *

Bethany parked where Casey indicated in front of a seedy government-subsidized apartment complex in Olympia. He grabbed the fish-filled cooler and headed toward a door. After knocking, he called, "It's me, Casey, Ms. Ladie."

The door cracked to allow an elderly African American woman to peer out. Seeing Casey, she opened the door fully. "What's this, baby?" she asked when Casey handed her several pounds of paper-wrapped fish.

"We brought you some salmon."

"Salmon? That's just for rich people."

Casey smiled. "Then today you're rich."

"Normally I bread and fry the squids you bring. How do you cook salmon?"

"Salmon is better baked. Maybe add a little seasoning salt on top. Take the fish out when the flakes separate."

"I'll try that." Ms. Ladie looked past Casey. "You brought a young lady with you." She stepped out of the doorway. "Please do come in. I've got iced tea."

"Sorry, Ms. Ladie. This is Bethany. But we can't stay. We've got a lot of fish to deliver."

Ms. Ladie hugged Casey and said, "God bless you, baby." She reached out to touch Bethany with a bony hand. "Promise you'll come back, honey."

Not knowing what to say, Bethany murmured, "I will."

"Ms. Ladie worked cooking and cleaning for a prominent wealthy family," Casey explained as they went to a different door. "But they paid her in cash without Social Security. She has no legally acceptable records to prove her employment. Now she's destitute."

"She still has legal recourse," Bethany insisted. "I'd bet that family would settle if faced with the embarrassment of a court action."

"That sounds like blackmail."

"No, that's leverage to get justice," returned Bethany. After a pause, she asked, "You take squid to Ms. Ladie?"

Casey looked embarrassed. "In late summer, you can snag them under spotlights off of piers. In a few hours, I can fill a five-gallon bucket. And there's great comradery on the pier. Squid have a lot of protein. I eat them myself, as well as give them away."

Lucia Hernandez answered the second door Casey knocked at. Five wide-eyed children aged two to ten clustered around her. "I've brought you some fish, Lucia, salmon and rockfish. You have a freezer, right?" asked Casey.

"We do have a freezer, Casey. Where did you get the fish?"

"Some friends and I caught them."

"Oh my. Thank you. I love fish and would love for my kids to try some."

"Can we bring the fish in?"

"Sí."

Bethany watched Casey move to an old refrigerator in the kitchen and squeeze as much fish as possible into the small freezer compartment. The children obviously knew him and tugged at his arms and legs to converse. Casey spoke to each by name and then hurried to leave. Lucia kissed both him and Bethany on the cheek as they departed.

Outside, Casey told Bethany, "Lucia is an American-born citizen. She married a hardworking man not knowing he had entered the country illegally. Long story short—he was falsely accused of shoplifting by a witness who couldn't tell one Latino from another and deported to Guatemala without a trial. He sends Lucia what money he can."

Before Bethany could comment, Casey approached and knocked on another door. A frail-looking Belarusian man appeared. Through the man's English-speaking daughter, Casey offered the fish.

The man smiled broadly, "Da, da. Spasibo."

After leaving plenty of fish, Casey told Bethany, "Dimitri was a doctor in Belarus. The family defected on a holiday trip and were granted asylum in the US. Then he was afflicted by a debilitating but non-fatal bowel problem. They have no money or insurance to pay for an operation. His wife supports the family working at a Dairy Queen restaurant."

Delivering all the fish took nearly two hours. Back in Bethany's car, Casey asked, "Have you ever thought about being an environmental lawyer or representing poor people in their dilemmas?"

"I like convicting bad guys."

"You heard about plenty of bad guys and injustices tonight. My blog could give you all the clients you want."

Bethany shrugged, then asked, "Are we close to your home? I'd like to see where you live."

Casey's face reflected dismay. "It's a dump."

"Doesn't mean I shouldn't see it."

With some persuasion, Casey agreed to show Bethany the room he rented in a large rundown house owned by an older Caucasian woman. Bethany found his room to be indeed cramped and modest but clean and well-ordered.

Chapter Seventeen

Early the next morning, buzzing woke Katie. She opened her cell phone. "Hello."

A gruff voice asked, "Is this the Alabama sportsman interested in a trophy?"

"That's my husband."

Katie shook sleeping Dave violently and whispered into his ear, "This is the call." She put the phone on speaker so she could listen, then thrust the phone into his hand.

Dave, unusual for his sleepyhead nature, reacted instantly. "To whom am I speaking?"

"No names for this transaction. And cash only. I understand you're looking for a special trophy?"

"Yes, I am. I entertain business associates at a place I own in—"

"What do you want?"

"Well, what are my choices?"

"I've got bearskin rugs, a couple of cured mountain lion skins with taxidermy head, wolf pelts, and a wolverine or two. You can have any already cured for five thousand. I've even got a tanned orca hide. But that's twenty thousand. A taxidermy bald eagle is only three thousand."

"My wife wanted a live bear cub."

"I got that too. A female. But only one. Five thousand for the cub."

"We'll take the cured mountain lion skin and the bear cub. Where do I meet you to collect them?"

"You don't. I'll have the merchandise delivered to Willis Boone's place in three days. You'll need to pay him a thousand for his trouble and the delivery man another thousand. So that comes to twelve thousand. You got that much?"

"I can get it."

"Remember, cash only. And you'll need a carrier for the bear." *Click.*

* * *

Katie took the phone and immediately called Aaron then handed the phone to Dave.

"We got the call just a few minutes ago. Did you record it?" Dave demanded of the voice that answered.

"Yeah, we got something. But it looks like a burner phone somewhere east of the Cascades," Aaron answered. "We do have a distinctive male voice recorded, though. That's worthwhile if we can identify the caller. Thanks for permission to tap your phone. But why did you ask to buy the bear cub? DFW can't pay for that."

"I didn't want it to end up providing fresh gall like the case you described. The cub is also proof of wildlife trafficking . . ." Katie paused, ". . . and a present for Denyse."

"Your daughter-in-law receiving the cub is illegal too."

"I don't mean she'll keep the cub. Denyse inherited a gentle-hearted nature from her mother and can't stand to see animals abused. She'll turn the cub over to the licensed animal rescue shelter where she left the raccoon. She made Jeremy pay fifty dollars each for three Douglas squirrels and then released them into the woods."

"Denyse sounds like a kind person."

"She is. But we're not done yet, Aaron."

"I didn't expect so."

"Can we have a Zoom call in an hour?"

"I'll be ready. Send me a link."

Dave hung up. "Is Casey's number in here, sweetheart?" he asked Katie while holding up her phone.

Katie took the phone and scrolled through her contacts, tapped Casey's number, then handed the phone back to Dave.

A sleepy male voice answered, "Hello."

In the background Dave heard a female voice ask, "Who is calling you this early on a Sunday?"

"It's Dave Parker," Casey said. "Dave, I'm putting you on speaker phone."

"Oh, hi, Dave. This is Bethany."

Dave looked at Katie, who shrugged. "Okay, Casey and Bethany, can you be ready for a Zoom conference in about an hour?"

"Sure," answered Casey. "What's up?"

"Important developments. I'll send a link and explain over Zoom."

* * *

Dave and Katie looked at themselves on the screen of Katie's laptop. A window opened to show Casey and Bethany together and looking disheveled in a decrepit bedroom. Then Jeremy and Denyse arrived on the call, even though they were only one hotel room away. Aaron joined last.

Dave started the meeting by clearing his throat then saying, "We've placed an order for a trophy and a live cub, hoping to identify the middleman." He recapped that morning's phone call.

Aaron injected a quip, "So what happened is that you and Katie baited the middleman."

"I guess you could say that. But we still don't have that man's identity. Here's what I propose we do to trace the illegal trophies and wildlife back to the source."

An hour later every detail of a plan had been hashed through.

Aaron and Casey would stake out Boone's house from the surrounding woods for the delivery of the mountain lion skin and bear cub. They would document the exchange and possibly identify the deliveryman. Bethany had resisted Casey's participation until Aaron assured her that he would be well armed and that Casey would be provided a bulletproof vest.

Jeremy and Denyse would supply food, water, spare batteries, and whatever was needed to Aaron and Casey. If caught, they would have the plausible excuse of looking to purchase more pets.

Bethany would stand by to access government records.

Dave and Katie would respond to the summons and collect the mountain lion skin and bear cub as evidence.

* * *

Katie had remained uncharacteristically quiet during the discussion. After everybody exited the meeting, Katie started, "Dave, I've been thinking."

"How is that news?"

Katie didn't acknowledge Dave's poor attempt at humor. "Do you remember Boone getting overexcited as you were about to shoot the bear?"

"I hardly remember any details. I was overcome with certainty that I didn't want to kill a bear, especially a mother bear."

"Well, Boone talked about the rifle being accurate. He said that it had killed a lot of animals, including a two-legged one who had tried to deny Boone his rights. What do you think he meant by that?"

Realization dawned on Dave. "Are you thinking about the missing DFW agent?"

"Could be."

"Get Aaron back on the phone."

Aaron answered immediately. "Yes, Dave."

"Katie remembered something, Aaron. We don't know if it's meaningful."

"Go on."

Dave gestured for Katie to speak. She told what she had heard that night. "I'm not sure what Boone meant. But it could refer to the missing DFW agent. Hal Dulfer, right?"

Aaron didn't speak for several seconds. His voice was grim. "Yes. Hal had two kids. He was my friend. If what you suspect is true, then we need to do everything necessary to discover and prove what happened. Then we can track down everyone who participated or knew."

"We're with you," said Dave. "That rifle could be linked to any number of crimes. It's hidden in the mountains. We might be able to find it."

"We also need ballistics from a bullet fired by that rifle."

"I know where we could find a bullet from that rifle," offered Katie. She explained her idea.

"Alright," said Aaron. "But we need to be very careful. Any of those militia adherents could be dangerous."

✳ ✳ ✳

Bethany swiped her buzzing phone. "Hello."

"This is Tara Moynihan from Redwood Hills, Bethany. You and Casey Carpenter helped me look for a location for a new store."

"Oh! I didn't expect you, Tara."

"Who are you expecting, Casey maybe?"

"No. Maybe. I don't know." Bethany sighed. "Casey is a great guy. But I don't know if there's a long-term future for us."

"He's head-over-heels for you, though."

"I know. But I just can't see how it could work out."

"That's too bad, because Casey is the reason I called."

"I can give you his number," Bethany offered.

"Jeff and I talked to Casey already. We signed a lease for a facility to open a new store called Outdoors Always in Olympia and offered Casey the manager position. But we haven't heard back from him. I thought you could . . . like, encourage him."

"You offered Casey a salaried job?"

"Sure. He's got a degree in business management. And we want the store to not only be a business, but to become a hub of outdoor activity and even advocacy. Casey could continue his blog. His Washington Coalition for Sustainability could have an office there. After the store became profitable, we'd talk about making Casey a part owner."

Bethany felt her stomach sink while wondering, *Why hasn't Casey mentioned this to me?* To Tara, she said, "That sounds like a remarkable opportunity."

"It is. Could you maybe nudge Casey a little in our direction? He trusts you. Talk some sense into him. Jeff and I can't afford lease payments without making progress toward an opening."

"Maybe Casey is preoccupied. The Parkers have made some major discoveries related to poaching and wildlife trafficking here in Washington."

Tara laughed. "That sounds just like Dave and Katie."

"Jeremy and Denyse are involved too and me," Bethany added. "But I'm reluctant to try influencing Casey, Tara. He has to make that decision himself."

"I'm no expert on relationships. But I do know that communication, especially about major decisions, is necessary."

"You're probably right. Thanks, Tara."

"Anytime."

Bethany hung up thinking, *Maybe Casey and I could have a future together if we can learn to communicate.*

Chapter Eighteen

"Thank you for taking me along again," said Sandra.

"You're welcome, Sandra. You deserve a day off from caring for Katelyn and David. And, as I recall, you found the bait site on our first trip up," answered Denyse.

"Are you sure the kids will be okay with Bethany?" asked Jeremy.

"Bethany won't be alone with the kids unless your parents have to leave to meet the middleman. That isn't likely today. And they liked Bethany on our day trip to Bainbridge Island. The question is whether Bethany will be okay. Two young kids can be a handful," said Denyse.

Jeremy laughed. "Yes, they can. You've done a wonderful job with them, Sandra. Maybe you should come home with us to Mobile."

Sandra felt her heart jump at Jeremy's unexpected idea. *That would be too good to actually happen,* she realized.

"But I know you'll be happy to get back to Melbourne," Jeremy casually added.

Rather than risk revealing her disappointment, Sandra said, "This is your third trip up this mountain. Will you show me where you camped?"

"You mean where we suffered for three days?" said Denyse. "Sure, I'll take you there while my stalwart husband digs for the bullet."

An hour later, Sandra stood looking at an uneven patch of bare ground where Denyse and Jeremy had waited. They could hear Jeremy's shovel scraping the ground three hundred feet away.

"This is where we took turns sleeping," explained Denyse. She foot-tapped the surface of a protruding boulder. "I tried to curl around this rock. We made hot water for tea and soup on a propane burner and watched the bait site from behind those trees." She pointed toward a clump of wind-stunted firs.

"I could use some help now," Jeremy called. His voice seemed loud in the stillness of the wilderness.

Denyse and Sandra hurried to find him at the large pile of decaying Douglas fir needles, soil, and gravel taken from the bear bait spot.

Denyse laid down a coarse wire sieve that Casey had borrowed from an archeologist. "So you want us to sift through all this until we find the bullet Dave shot?"

"Right. I'll hold the sieve and shake it. You can shovel in the loose dirt. Sandra can spread the dirt and throw out rocks. If it becomes too tedious, we can change jobs."

After a long hour and a half passed, Sandra picked a pebble off the wire screen that seemed heavier than others of the approximate size. She held it up to examine and saw a mushroom-shaped object. "Could this be a bullet?"

Jeremy laid down the sieve and took the object from her hand while Denyse stood poised with another shovel load. He held the object up between his index finger and thumb. "This is certainly a bullet. We're lucky it's an old-fashioned lead bullet and not a hollow-point that could have disintegrated." He held the bullet for Denyse and Sandra to see.

Denyse laid down the shovel. "How would they match that to anything?"

Jeremy pointed to the undistorted base. "By microscopic rifling marks. Each rifle makes a slightly unique pattern, like a fingerprint."

"What is rifling?" asked Sandra.

"They put a slight spiral inside the gun barrel. It makes the bullet spin in flight and go straighter."

"So we have the bullet?" asked Denyse.

"Probably," answered Jeremy as he put the bullet into a plastic zip top bag. He glanced back at the pile of dirt. "But we should finish sifting to make certain."

Denyse gave him a severe look and rolled her eyes but picked up the shovel. "My thorough husband."

Jeremy smiled. "Weren't you eager to join this case? Most detective work is tedious."

"I know."

An hour later, Denyse delivered the last shovelful. "Are we finished now?"

"Yes. I'm glad to be done too," Jeremy agreed.

Sandra watched Jeremy and Denyse interacting while working together. *I hope I can be married like this one day. Being with them in Alabama would be wonderful. But I'll have to go back to Australia soon.*

* * *

Bethany helped Katie prepare sandwiches for Katelyn and David's supper while the children watched *Bluey* in Denyse and Jeremy's hotel room. Bethany initiated another conversation. "I think a couple needs more than feelings and emotions to get through tough times together, especially to sustain a marriage. They need to anticipate a life together."

Katie cut the sandwiches diagonally and placed them on paper plates. "That is certainly true, honey. I wish more young women and men thought that through."

"Casey is fun, and I might even love him. He's been offered a real job. But he hasn't accepted it."

Katie put the sandwiches in front of the children. "Have you told Casey you think he should take the job?"

"He doesn't know that I know. I wish I didn't."

Katie gave lidded cups with straws and diluted apple juice to Katelyn and David. "Why do you wish you didn't know?"

"I'm not sure. Maybe because it's an unknown factor. Maybe because I'll be disappointed if he doesn't accept."

"Dave didn't make much money the first years of our marriage forty-six years ago. I supported us teaching. He insisted on a stringent budget with the money I made. No borrowing money except eventually for our house. Today we cherish the memory of those lean years. His budgeting and hard work establishing a business eventually made us reasonably well off."

"Because you had a dream and did it together, right?"

"Yes, we did."

"I just don't know if Casey—"

A knock on the door cut Bethany off. "Boone called, Katie. We need to leave now," Dave said through the door.

Katie looked at Bethany and gestured toward the children. "They're all yours, honey."

"Before you go, what should I do?"

"Let them watch TV and eat supper. Read them one of the books Denyse brought. Katelyn should be fine going to the bathroom by herself. You might need to set David on the seat after they eat and encourage him."

"Thanks. But I meant, what to do about Casey?"

"Make a good choice like you agreed Jeremy did."

"Should I tell Casey I know about Tara's offer?"

"You should encourage him somehow to voluntarily tell you. Keeping secrets isn't good for a relationship."

Bethany looked back at David and Katelyn after Katie closed the door behind herself. They continued staring at the screen. *I'll be okay as long as* Bluey *lasts.*

Twenty minutes later, Bluey signed off. After Katelyn went to the bathroom she said, "David needs to go too."

Bethany felt a surge of trepidation. "I'll bet you could help me with David."

"Okay."

Bethany cleaned up a juice spill while Katelyn took care of David. Then Bethany held up a book and offered, "Shall we read together?"

But both children were full of energy after watching TV. David began chasing Katelyn, who raced around the room dodging her little brother while both children laughed. When Katelyn scampered over the bed, David tried to follow, fell, and bumped his nose. When he started to cry, Bethany picked him up. "There, there. I know it hurts." She sat down on the couch with him in her lap. As David's cries turned to sniffles, Katelyn came to sit with them. Bethany reached for the book and started to read.

After a few minutes, David nodded off to sleep. Katelyn leaned against Bethany. Soon she fell asleep as well.

Feeling their warmth and closeness, Bethany thought, *This is really something. I'll bet Casey would be a good father.*

Eventually Bethany's arms began to ache. But she didn't stir. *Better to let them sleep.*

The sound of the hotel room door opening came as a relief. Denyse and Jeremy entered, followed by Sandra.

"Where's Katie?" whispered Denyse.

"She had to go meet Boone."

Denyse picked up Katelyn and carried her to the bed. Sandra took David to a mattress pad on the floor, leaving Bethany with Jeremy.

"Did you find the bullet?" she asked.

Jeremy handed her the zip top bag with the bullet. "We think so."

Bethany looked at the bullet. "Not a hollow point. Rifling on the butt end should be discernable."

* * *

Casey and Aaron waited while lying concealed in the woods after sunset near Boone's log cabin.

"If Katie was right about what she heard Boone say, this could lead to finding a killer . . . a killer in that cabin," said Casey in a voice barely above a whisper.

Aaron sighed. "I've got to find Hal and finish that case. I promised his wife. I've been so focused on following up any possible lead or hunch that I've neglected my family. I haven't taken my kids fishing or my wife out to dinner all summer. Helen understands, but she feels abandoned and is running out of patience. Many officers at DFW struggle with being workaholics because they love and believe in their jobs. But I've . . ." Aaron trailed off.

"You're carrying a heavy burden, alright." After a silence, Casey continued, "I wish I could have a family—a family like yours or the Parkers."

Aaron whispered back, "Family is the way to go. The best life you can live." After a pause, Aaron continued, "You need to provide for a family, though. And let me tell you, kids are expensive."

"I don't know if Bethany wants—" A text arriving on Casey's phone interrupted him. After reading it, Casey said, "Katie says she and Dave are on their way. The exchange is supposed to be at about eleven. That's an hour from now."

Aaron looked at his own phone. "I've got the same. It's dark enough now. Let's get closer. Feel your way slowly on your hands and knees."

Twenty minutes later, Aaron and Casey lay still among some alder trees at the edge of the graveled parking area. They froze in their camouflage clothes when a nondescript van's headlights swept above them. Dogs began to bark from behind the cabin. A dim porch light came on and the cabin's front door opened. A man recognizable as Boone emerged carrying an AR-15.

"Jeremiah Johnson!" shouted Boone. "Good to see you. I got the dogs tied up out back."

A man wearing a militia patch got out of the van also carrying an automatic rifle. "Good to see you, Boone." The two men shared a hearty handshake. "Our captain says we'll both get a thousand tonight."

"The buyers should be here at eleven. 'Bout thirty minutes from now. Come on in and have a beer." The two men went through the front door. Then the porch light went out.

Casey heard Aaron whisper, "We need to track that van." Aaron stood up. "Quickly now. While the dogs are still making noise that will cover us. You get the tag number like we planned. If anything goes wrong, run like hell down the driveway. Don't stop if you hear shots fired."

Casey heard the light crunch of gravel as Aaron stood and crossed the parking area to the van. *Will they hear my heart beating?* Casey asked himself as he followed. Aaron lay down on his back and inched underneath the van. Casey found the license tag and traced the numbers and letters in the dark with his fingers, mentally recording them. Aaron wriggling out from under the van interrupted his third check. He followed Aaron back to the woods edge.

"You get the tag number?" whispered Aaron.

"I'll remember it for the rest of my life."

Aaron stifled a chuckle. "You did well. I've got the tracker attached too."

Twenty-five minutes later a vehicle Casey recognized as the Parkers' rental came slowly up Boone's driveway. The SUV stopped in front of the house and remained running. The porch light came on and two men came outside into the headlights carrying AR-15s. Casey could barely hear Aaron snapping photos of Boone and Johnson in the light.

"Cut off those headlights," demanded Boone.

The headlights went dark. Dave opened the SUV's passenger-side door and stepped onto the gravel.

"You got twelve thousand in cash?" called Boone.

"I do," answered Dave.

Casey heard Aaron click the safety off his automatic pistol to intervene if necessary.

"Captain said to check them for a wire just to be careful," Boone told Johnson.

After fumbling his hands over Dave then Katie, Johnson stepped back. "Clean."

Boone lowered his gun and spoke to Dave. "Now, hand over the twelve thousand."

"I need to see what I'm getting first."

Boone gestured to Johnson, who opened the van's sliding door, pulled out a beige rolled-up animal skin with a taxidermy head of a mountain lion, and handed it to Dave.

Dave started to unroll the skin. "What about the bear?"

Johnson returned to the van, fumbled for a minute, and brought out a cub, which squalled at being manhandled by its neck.

Suddenly, the headlights came back on, illuminating Boone, Dave, the house, the mountain lion pelt, and Johnson holding the cub. Aaron's camera snapped several times documenting the exchange.

"I said no lights!" shouted Boone and pointed his rifle at the SUV.

Chapter Nineteen

The headlights went dark again. Katie spilled out of the driver's side door with the animal carrier purchased for Denyse's raccoon. "I'm sorry," she said. "I just wanted to see the little cub. Would you put her in here?" she asked Johnson, who roughly shoved the eleven-pound animal into the carrier. Katie took the cub and returned to the SUV's driver's seat.

Boone lowered his rifle. "Alright, now let's have the money."

Dave reached into his jacket pocket and pulled out a thick sheaf of hundred-dollar bills. "Here. Do you want me to count them out?"

"I'll do that," Boone insisted. He pulled a small flashlight from his pocket and proceeded to count to a hundred and twenty. "That'll do."

Dave nodded and returned to the passenger side with the lion skin. Katie backed the SUV to turn around. Only when facing down the driveway and past where she anticipated Casey and Aaron to be hiding did she turn on the headlights.

Casey heard Boone and Johnson chortling. "You scared the hell out of them," said Johnson.

"Damned rich tourists deserved it. Want another beer?"

"I'll take it with me."

"Okay. Here's a thousand for you and for me. You'll deliver ten thousand to our captain."

"Right."

After a minute, the van departed and Boone went back inside. The dogs continued to bark. Casey heard Aaron exhale and click the pistol back on safety. "Okay. You walk to the highway and text the Parkers to pick us up. I'll collect our stuff from the woods and join you," said Aaron.

Ten minutes later Dave and Katie picked up Casey and Aaron then headed back to Bremerton. Dave's voice revealed regret. "Johnson struck me as being a lackey. I think Boone's accomplice was just a go-between, and not the actual middleman. Bosses of criminal enterprises frequently avoid attending incriminating transactions."

"I took what should be air-tight incriminating photos of Boone and Johnson, though," responded Aaron. "We should be able to follow Johnson's movements using the GPS tracker. Someplace he goes in the next few days should lead us to his boss."

Denyse, Jeremy, Bethany, and Sandra waited in the Baymont. After midnight they heard a light knock on the hotel room door and opened it to see Katie standing in the hallway. "Come to our room," said Katie quietly.

"I'll stay with the children," Sandra volunteered.

Next door, Jeremy, Denyse, and Bethany found Casey and Aaron along with Dave and Katie clustered around an animal carrier. "She looks torpid," said Katie.

"Probably malnourished," replied Aaron.

Bethany surprised Casey with a lingering hug when he turned to greet them.

Denyse leaned over to look at the small bear huddled in a corner. "I'll feed her right now. Jeremy, please get the raccoon's bottle, milk, and cream."

After the mixture had been microwave warmed, Denyse wrapped the pathetic little bear in a towel to hold in her lap. The group watched her pry the tiny animal's mouth open by pressing on the spot where her jaws met and squirting a little milk onto her tongue. After four attempts like this, the little bear got the idea and began to suck.

Everybody in the hotel room sighed with relief.

Jeremy spoke first. "This hotel has a policy of no dogs or cats. I wonder what they'd say about a bear?"

"Let's not find out," answered Katie.

Aaron spoke for DFW, "Please take her to a licensed wildlife facility in the morning."

"Sure. After we feed her breakfast," returned Denyse. "I want my children and Sandra to see her."

"Fair enough."

While the little bear gorged itself, everybody recited their stories. Finally, at nearly two in the morning, Bethany said, "I've got to work tomorrow," and departed. Aaron drove Casey back to Olympia where they both lived. After the little bear fell asleep in Denyse's lap, she transferred her to the carrier. All the Parkers slept soundly.

* * *

"I'm getting to know this trail well," said Denyse as she and everybody but Katie and the kids trudged skyward.

Jeremy nodded in sympathy. "You and me both. This is our fourth time up."

"First time for me," said Bethany. "But I really want to find that rifle. It could link Boone to the slugs that have been found in mutilated bear carcasses. I took a day of vacation to do this."

"Why isn't the bullet we dug up enough?" asked Denyse.

Aaron answered for Bethany. "Because a defense lawyer could argue that bullet had been fired from a different rifle at another time. We can't prove that bullet was the one Dave fired."

Dave stopped on the trail. "This is the place where Boone left us to retrieve the rifle. I recognize that rock." He gestured to the left. "Boone went that way and met us farther up the trail with the rifle. Let's make a line with Aaron on one end and Casey on the other. Then we can sweep uphill and to our right. The rifle is sealed in clear plastic wrap. It's probably under a boulder or other place hidden and partially protected from the weather."

Denyse found herself missing the open trail as she tried to work around fallen trees and loose rocks. She kept glancing to remain in line with Sandra on her right and Jeremy on her left. *I'm just glad these mountains have no venomous snakes,* she thought.

An hour later on the group's fourth sweep, a reflection attracted Denyse's eye. She looked closer. Under a toppled tree trunk, rocks had been piled. A corner of protruding plastic had caught a glimmer of sunlight. "I might have something here," she called to the others. Starting with Jeremy and Sandra, the group converged on her.

Denyse pointed at the exposed corner. Jeremy knelt and started removing the rocks. As all watched, the stock of a plastic-wrapped rifle appeared. Jeremy stepped back and said, "Aaron, this is evidence. A law enforcement officer should take charge now."

"Thank you, Jeremy," said Aaron as he finished the excavation then put on gloves and pulled a larger plastic bag from his knapsack. Gingerly he put the rifle still wrapped in plastic into the larger bag.

"The plastic wrap itself could be evidence," explained Bethany. "I expect that we'll find Boone's fingerprints on the plastic and the rifle. Dave's fingerprints should only be on the rifle. That would confirm Dave's story and will be impossible to refute in court."

"Good eye to spot that, Denyse," said Dave. Everybody then congratulated Denyse in a mood of jubilation.

"We've got the rest of the day ahead of us," said Casey. "Anybody up for a hike?"

"I need to get this rifle to the police lab," answered Aaron.

The Parkers and Sandra looked at each other. "I've had enough trail for now," said Dave. The others murmured agreement. "Let's go collect Katie and the kids and go out to dinner together."

"Lead the way, Dad," answered Jeremy.

"I'll hike with you, Casey," said Bethany.

* * *

Casey felt elated. The rifle had been found. He reveled in the majestic wonder of the mountains. And best of all, the woman he loved was sharing those experiences with him. The only negative was that although hiking with him, Bethany seemed preoccupied. "What are you thinking about?" he asked.

Bethany turned around to face Casey on the trail. "I'm thinking about us."

Casey's heart soared before some concern crept in. "How?"

"I'm wondering what a life together might look like."

"Here's another consideration. Tara called me, Bethany. She wants me to manage a big store in Olympia. The store would also serve as a base for our sustainability efforts. But that would put me in

Olympia and you in Seattle. You know what the I-5 traffic is like on weekdays. Because of that, I haven't decided yet. I should have told you about the job offer earlier."

Bethany nodded. "Tara called me too. But I wanted to give you a chance to tell me about her offer yourself. Maybe I should have told you about her call. Regardless, if we were to ever marry, neither of us should keep secrets."

Casey nodded agreement. "Okay. What do you think about the job?"

"I think it's a great opportunity for you. The chance of a lifetime. But you need to decide for yourself, Casey. I do realize that if you take that position, you'll be in Olympia while my job is in Seattle. That could limit a future we might have together."

Casey's heart soared at Bethany's reference to a future together. "You're more important to me than any job."

"I believe you feel that way, Casey. But building a life together also needs practicalities. I want to live with a husband, in the same place, with better than a minimum-wage income."

The implications of her words sobered Casey. "So we're doomed regardless of what I decide?"

"I wouldn't say that. Not yet." Bethany kissed Casey and smiled. "Now that we've communicated about our mutual circumstance, I can fully enjoy our hike."

Maybe you can, thought Casey.

* * *

With the tracker planted to identify the middleman and the rifle located, Dave announced, "The investigation is in Aaron's hands now."

"Does that mean we have to go home now?" asked Denyse.

Sandra's heart sank at the possibility of going back to Australia.

Katie answered for her husband, "Not by a long shot. When Aaron and other law enforcement authorities issue warrants and start making arrests, they'll certainly need us for depositions and arraignment testimony. We can't possibly leave now."

Sandra felt relief.

"So we've got free time on our hands again," suggested Jeremy. "What shall we do?"

A long silence followed. To everybody's surprise, especially Sandra's, Dave turned to her. "You've been a tremendous help to us, Sandra. What would you like to do?"

Sandra saw everybody looking at her expectantly. Her mind raced to the tourist brochures from the hotel lobby she had read while Katelyn and David slept. "I have never been on a boat over the water. I read about a boat that goes from Washington to a town in Canada called Victoria."

"I've never been to Canada," said Denyse.

"None of us have," added Katie. "We all brought our passports, right?"

After seeing everybody nod, Denyse googled Victoria. "Look. Victoria is a lovely town."

"See if you can get us a hotel reservation for overnight," said Dave.

"Great idea, Sandra," said Jeremy.

* * *

Sandra sat admiring the snow-covered Olympic Mountains from onboard the Black Ball Ferry returning across the Strait of Juan de Fuca from Victoria, British Columbia, to Port Angeles. Jeremy and Denyse played little games with their children at a booth nearby. Dave alternated reading about the American western migration and nodding off to sleep due to the warmth of the sun shining through the windows and the gentle roll and rumble of the boat.

Sandra smiled when Katie came to sit next to her. "Thank you for taking me with your family to Canada." A few tears ran down her cheeks. "You have been so good to me."

"It was your idea. Besides, the Parkers, the Larkins—Denyse's parents and brother—and the Travnikovs are all a family now. You and I are both part of that family, honey."

Denyse learned to call people "honey" from Katie, Sandra realized. *It's a term of endearment from American Southern women. Like Luv is among some Australian women.* "Thank you, Mrs. Parker. I mean Katie."

"We're just happy to get to know you, Sandra. We love your sister Lena."

"Lena thinks you and Dave are wonderful. She enjoys telling the story of you finding her with her baby when they were homeless."

"Lena revealing that Denyse's brother, Trevor, was her husband certainly surprised us."

"Denyse's father, Dingo, likes to show the video clip of Dave punching Lena's kidnapper. He also shows the video of a big fight at Denyse and Jeremy's wedding. There Dave got punched."

Katie laughed. "Yes, Dave did. Dingo nearly caused us big trouble when he gave those clips to a TV station where we live. But we think God turned it to something good."

"Dingo said that Dave shot a man with a gun once. He came back for a mate . . . to save a policeman. Is that true?"

"Yes. I was there and saw it. Being forced to do that caused Dave nightmares for years afterwards, though."

"Well, Dingo is proud of Dave. He calls Dave a 'hero' and a 'real bloke.'"

"I know you've had some hard times too, honey. Your father was murdered. Then the murderers stole your parents' farm?"

"Yes. That was part of the war with Russia. We walked for weeks as refugees. Then Lena went to New Zealand to make money for us. When we were starving and needed money for medicine, men offered Mama money for me. But not as much money as they offered for Sveta."

"Why more for Sveta?"

"She is very pretty. In Australia, every man wants her as his girlfriend or wife. I'm just a Ukrainian peasant girl."

Katie's voice grew stern. "Don't say that, Sandra. God makes every person special. I understand you're very smart. The best men—the men who want a good woman for a lifetime—know that youthful prettiness passes."

"How will men know that I'm a good woman if they never talk to me? They're busy crowding around Sveta like bees to sugar water. They don't even notice me. Sveta never thinks about Ukraine anymore. I think of Ukraine all the time."

Katie considered that and admitted, "Young men *can* be shallow." She took a long look at Sandra. "Your long straight hair doesn't fit your round face. You should try a shorter cut with a little curl. Your mouth is cute. You could accent that with a tiny bit of lipstick."

"A lot of women in Ukraine use dark red lipstick."

"In America and probably Australia, the trick is to look like you're not wearing any makeup. Your complexion is so good that you wouldn't need much.

And, Sandra, you should smile showing your nice teeth. See how Denyse smiles? Scowling women might look sexy to some men. But a smiling woman looks like she would make a good wife."

Sandra sat amazed. "Nobody has ever told me these things."

"I'm from the South, honey. Southern women take appearances seriously." Katie pointed at Denyse again. "See her long face? She wears her hair long to fit but puts it into a ponytail to make her look cute and athletic rather than alluring. Look how she's plucked her eyebrows just a little and lightly highlighted her eyes without looking made up."

"Would you help me, Katie?"

"I can give you some tips. But you'll also need to experiment and discover what works for you."

Chapter Twenty

"Washington keeps surpassing itself," said Katie on a mountaintop after their return to the US. "I've never seen such a magnificent view."

"Me neither," agreed Denyse. "I wonder why the tourist guides don't make a big deal about Deer Park. There's hardly anyone here, although this is in Olympic National Park."

"There are no facilities to support large crowds," suggested Dave. "And the access along that narrow, winding, unpaved road is a deterrent. Hurricane Ridge is much easier for tourists. This is primarily a parking spot for backpackers."

Jeremy pointed north. "There's the Strait of Juan de Fuca we crossed to get to Victoria." His arm swung in a clockwise arc to the right. "I can see the entire Salish Sea, Puget Sound, and the Hood Canal as if we were in an airplane."

"You'd never see such a view through a tiny airline window, though. Maybe in a helicopter with a clear bubble windshield," said Denyse.

Jeremy nodded. "Maybe." He then continued his arm sweep around to the south. "And from the same spot, we see a panorama of the snow-covered Olympic Mountains. There's Mount Rainier in the distance. This is unbelievable."

"Yeah, it is," agreed Dave. "I'm glad you insisted we follow that inconspicuous sign, Denyse."

"I hoped the kids would see some deer," she replied. "This is better."

Sandra held little David in her arms. "Thank you for bringing me here."

* * *

Three days after the recovery of the rifle, Katie's phone rang. She answered and hearing Aaron's voice put the phone on speaker to include Dave. Aaron's tone revealed the seriousness of the call.

"Dave and Katie, fingerprinting by the police lab has tied Boone to both the plastic wrapping and rifle. As Bethany predicted, Dave's fingerprints are only on the rifle itself, confirming your story. My presence within hearing range of the setup allows me to further corroborate with you. Ballistics testing of the rifle confirms that the bullet recovered came from that 30-30 and matches bullets recovered from several poached bears. We have Boone cold on poaching. Since this has all occurred on federal lands, national forest, and in Olympic National Park, we'll need to involve their officers going forward." Aaron paused.

"What about Boone's partner, Brian Manning?" asked Dave.

"The photos you took of them packing food to the bait site ties him in as an accomplice to poaching."

"Did you locate the one they call Captain?" asked Katie.

"I'm getting to that," answered Aaron. "The van used to deliver the lion pelt and bear cub to Boone's cabin is registered to Jeremiah Johnson. The most fervent Pioneer Spirit Militia members have legally changed their names to that of famous American pioneers. Johnson used to be Cecil Gilequest." Aaron sighed. "Anyway, the tracker shows Johnson driving the van to a ranch east of the Cascades and stopping there for fifteen minutes. Then Johnson drove to his home in Ellensburg. The owner of the ranch is Andrew Jackson, formally Clyde Stansky. The FBI in Olympia keeps a large file on Pioneer Spirit Militia.

They confirm that militia members call Jackson 'Captain' and that the militia frequently conducts what they call 'drills' on his ranch."

Dave and Katie looked at each other. Dave raised his arms like a football referee signaling a touchdown. Katie bowed her head, thanking God.

Aaron continued, "The reason I'm calling right now is that DFW is cooperating with the Washington State Police. We're going to execute search and arrest warrants at Jackson's ranch northeast of Wenatchee and at Boone's cabin early tomorrow morning. We'd like to hire Dave as a forensic accountant to examine financial records that might be seized. The Jackson house is the most likely place to locate incriminating records. You'd go into the house as soon as officers have secured it so that any leads you might find could be immediately pursued before word goes out on the militia grapevine. Also, there might be money related to a criminal enterprise that should be frozen or confiscated."

"Because I've been involved in the crime investigation, I couldn't testify as an independent expert in court," responded Dave.

"We'll get another forensic accountant if expert testimony is necessary. Right now, we need somebody good and fast to identify the leads and money before they disappear."

"Where is Wenatchee?"

"East of the Cascades on the Columbia River. That's the heart of Washington's apple-growing region. A three to four hour drive from your hotel. I could pick you up in a DFW vehicle, and Katie too if she's willing to come. We'd drive through the night and be in a support position tomorrow morning."

Dave looked at Katie, who nodded her head vigorously. "What time do you want us to be ready?"

* * *

At an assembly point a few miles from Jackson's ranch, Aaron told the searchers about the possible connection of the militia to Hal Dulfer's disappearance. "Seize everything that might be incriminating for animal trafficking. But especially look for anything that might allude to Hal."

Just before dawn, a convoy of police vehicles and a couple of FBI agents sped to Jackson's ranch house. Aaron and several state police hurried to the front door. A short, stocky man in his mid-fifties confronted them there. "What is this about?"

"We have a search warrant for this premises and an arrest warrant for Andrew Jackson. Are you Andrew Jackson?"

"Yes. But you have no right—"

"You are under arrest on suspicion of wild animal trafficking," Aaron interrupted then proceeded to read the legal rights.

After an officer led Jackson in handcuffs to a patrol car, a gaunt woman appeared on the front porch. "I didn't change my name to Jackson. I'm Wilma Stansky, Andrew's wife. He has been physically abusing me and wouldn't let me and our three kids leave. I want to fully cooperate."

"If you're cooperating, show us your husband's financial records," returned Aaron.

"This way." Leading the officers downstairs, she explained, "I don't want my kids taken by the state. We'll also need witness protection." She turned on bright lights in an open basement.

In the well-lit space, Aaron saw shelves laden with rolled-up animal pelts, bear paws, and other marketable animal parts he couldn't recognize. A handwritten logbook lay open on a large, cluttered desk. A desktop computer sat in the midst of the clutter. "Do you have a password for the computer?" asked Aaron.

"It's 'PioneerSpirit,' no spaces, with the P and S capitalized. That's the name of Andrew's militia. His 'private army,' I call them. Two militiamen he employs as ranch hands and calls 'officers' stay in the barn's apartment."

Aaron turned to one of the state troopers. "Would you bring in Dave Parker? He and his wife are waiting in my car."

Casey entered the double doors of McDonald's not far from his room in Olympia. He looked around for Bethany and waved when he saw her.

"McDonald's is a strange place to meet," he said while slipping into a booth opposite her. "What's going on?"

"We need to talk. I mean talk seriously in a place where hormones won't take over."

"Alright. Are you hungry? Should we order something?"

"Maybe later."

Casey sensed tension in Bethany's voice. *She's breaking up with me,* he thought. *But maybe not. She did say, "Maybe later." She hasn't planned to dump me and leave.* "Talk about what? The case?"

Bethany gave him an exasperated look. "About you and me."

"I know that Tara's job offer complicates our situation. Jobs in different cities. But I think you know how I feel about you. I'm in love with you, Bethany. I respect you and would like us to have a family together."

Bethany hesitantly smiled. "I love you too, Casey. But I'm afraid. You know I was married once before. That was awful. Losing a baby made it worse. I like what we have already and don't want to risk that."

"I understand. But I think we could have something even better. A life together with deeper love, companionship, and partnership."

"Plus different values, arguments, hurt feelings, and twice life's troubles because we would each bring our own issues into the marriage."

Casey smiled. "Those things too. But having a family . . . a family like the Parkers would make it all worthwhile."

"Whether you take the job or not, I honestly don't see any path forward for us. You need to make that decision without the pressure of wondering how I might react. I wanted to settle our relationship today so you could make an uninfluenced decision."

"So is this a proposal or a breakup?" Casey fidgeted while Bethany delayed.

"Maybe it's time I took a risk on something I can't prove in court," Bethany said softly, seemingly to herself. Finally, she looked him in the eyes. "It's a proposal, if you want it."

Casey leaned back. "This isn't the romantic moment I had imagined."

"I'm a lawyer. We're pragmatic." Bethany's quip lightened the atmosphere.

"Are you going to have me sign a contract to love you forever? If so, I'll sign."

Bethany's serious face softened into a smile. "Love me forever among other male responsibilities such as opening jar lids."

The couple stared at each other for a long minute until Casey said, "So we're getting married?"

"Yes . . . we . . . are. I suppose you'd like to go to your room now."

"No. I'd like to start communicating about the life we can share. Let's start looking for a path forward together. First, what do you really think about the job Tara and Jeff offered me? Should I take it?"

"Okay, we'll discuss that. Then we'll talk about my career. Should I stay at my steady job with Seattle's DA or open a practice, maybe in Olympia, championing the little guys and environmental issues? After that we can discuss where to live and if or when to try having kids."

"Now let's get some food and plan while we eat."

"This is a good way to start," said Bethany.

* * *

A man knocked on the window of Aaron's DFW vehicle where Katie and Dave waited. Dave lowered the glass. "You're needed inside now," said a state trooper.

Katie followed Dave into the ranch house. In the kitchen, she saw a bedraggled woman fixing breakfast for three frightened children. Around the house, men and women officers opened drawers and poked through closets. The trooper led her and Dave downstairs.

Aaron waited for them there. He pointed to a logbook and a computer. "Please just do the best you can quickly. I've already opened the computer for you."

Dave immediately started with the logbook. "Katie, would you please try to find me a Coca-Cola?"

Katie went back upstairs to the kitchen. She spoke to the mother struggling to calm and feed her children. "Would you have a Coca-Cola I could buy?"

"Some are in the refrigerator. Help yourself," the woman answered.

Katie found several cans of cold classic Coke. She carried one to Dave, who grunted, "Thanks," but didn't take his eyes away from the logbook.

Katie looked around the basement. She saw Aaron and a female DFW officer looking outraged while unrolling a black and white pelt. A third angry officer snapped pictures.

She heard Aaron say, "This accounts for the missing orcas."

Being near three furious law officers didn't appeal to Katie. She returned to the kitchen. The oldest child, a girl of about eight, had started to cry. A fussing toddler sat in a highchair with a bowl of warm oatmeal and a spoon waiting. Katie sat down, picked up the spoon, and asked the mother, "Do you mind?"

The woman glanced away from the eight-year-old she was attempting to comfort. "Be my guest."

Katie cooed and held the spoon before the little boy's mouth. He opened, swallowed, and settled down.

The stressed mother looked at Katie feeding her son. "Are you from Family Services?"

"No. I'm actually just visiting Washington. My husband downstairs is an accountant. My name is Katie Parker."

"Wilma Stansky, here. Thank you for your help. We're having a hard morning. Nine hard years, actually."

After a few minutes, the toddler tired of oatmeal. Katie saw a box of Cheerios in a cupboard. She gestured to Wilma, who nodded. Katie sprinkled a few before the child, who immediately started fisting them toward his mouth.

"Could I make you some coffee, Wilma?"

"Yes, please."

Chapter Twenty-one

Forty-five minutes later, Dave interrupted Aaron, who was working on documenting the illicit trophies. "You said to work quickly. Let me tell you what I've found so far."

"Please do."

"First, we're in luck." Dave opened the first page of Jackson's logbook. "Here are the usernames and passwords to all of Jackson's accounts. I checked his local bank account already. We know that all local transactions were handled in cash. Then the bank records show frequent cash deposits under ten thousand dollars, which the bank wouldn't be required to report. Checks drawn on the local bank paid for the ranch mortgage and living expenses. The bank shows no other sources of income, such as cattle sales from the ranch.

"I also found an offshore bank account showing international deposits presumably from customers. There's about four hundred twenty thousand dollars there. That will take some court work but is likely recoverable."

Aaron patted Dave on the back. "Nice work."

"That's not all." Dave turned to another section in the logbook. "This is a record of local cash transactions. Names, amounts, and merchandise are listed. From the amounts, I'd think that there's about two hundred fifty thousand in cash hidden somewhere. That's in addition to ten to twenty thousand dollars I found." Dave opened a drawer in the desk filled with hundred-dollar bills. "The remainder is probably in a cache nearby. All this money should be subject to civil forfeiture."

Dave heard a sharp intake of breath from Aaron. "The money is good," said Aaron. "But I'm more interested in arresting perpetrators."

"Then you'll like this." Dave turned to the computer and pulled up a spreadsheet. "This is a list of the Pioneer Spirit Militia members, Jackson's likely suppliers. Names, addresses, and contact information are here. Correlate these with the transactions listed in the logbook and you'll have plenty of perpetrators. You know about the animal trafficking, and I see you inventorying the illegal trophies. In addition, the records would indicate that Pioneer Militia had members rustling timber, setting illegal salmon traps, and even dealing in stolen vehicle parts.

"And maybe even better . . ." Dave brought up another spreadsheet on the computer. "These are Jackson's customers. Many of them dealt with Jackson through his offshore account. I found one payment of a hundred thousand dollars from 'AS.' Something pretty significant, I'm guessing. My work here is quick, but not thorough."

Dave continued, "As I said, as part of the investigation, I can't be your legal expert in court. The state will need to hire a forensic accounting firm."

"You'd be adequate for arrest warrants and arraignments, though?" asked Aaron.

"Sure."

* * *

Denyse sat in the back seat with Katelyn and David listening to her husband bantering with Sandra and thinking, *Jeremy doesn't realize Sandra has a crush on him. He's just being friendly and courteous. He'll make her aspire to marry a good man. And talking with a young man is good practice for her. I'm glad I put her in the front seat.*

"Another half hour and we'll be in Forks, the vampire capital of the world," announced Jeremy while driving on Highway 101. "Would you like to take a walk in the woods, Bella—I mean Sandra?"

Sandra smiled, showing her teeth. "I might meet my true love there." Sandra looked through the windshield. "The woods do look creepy. All that moss on the trees."

"That's because Forks is the rainiest town in our forty-eight contiguous states. It averages eleven feet of rain each year," explained Denyse from the back seat while looking at her phone. "Where we're staying in Bremerton is in what they call the rain shadow of the Olympic Mountains. Only four feet of precipitation all year."

"If your true love turned out to be a vampire, what would your children be?" wondered Jeremy.

Sandra shuddered. "Even more creepy."

"I'm guessing a tax collector," said Jeremy.

"Or a lawyer," Sandra came back.

"You'd both be wrong," Denyse announced. "The children would be dhampirs."

Jeremy met Denyse's eyes through the rearview mirror. "How do you know that?"

Denyse held up her cell phone. "Google. Dhampirs eat regular food, can see invisible vampires, and often make a career as vampire hunters."

"Look at the bright side, Sandra. With your kids' careers already laid out, you wouldn't need to save up to send them to college."

"Unless one decided to be a lawyer."

Jeremy laughed. "Good answer." Then he asked, "Does Ukraine have colorful folklore?"

"We had the mavkas. Those are the spirits of girls who had tragic deaths. They appear as beautiful young women who lure young men into the woods and kill them by tickling."

"What would happen if a mavka met a vampire in the woods?"

"The mavka would become a female lawyer who makes criminals die laughing."

After groaning at Sandra's clever reply, Jeremy asked, "What ethnicity are Ukrainians?"

"We are Slavic, of course. My family also descended from the Cossacks. They were fierce warriors who defended Ukraine against Turkey and the Tatars. But they were mostly independent. Wouldn't obey any government."

"You should be proud of that heritage."

"I never thought about that. But I should."

Denyse enjoyed observing Sandra blossom while conversing with Jeremy. *I've never seen Sandra so confident. That perky short hairstyle and cute outfit Katie paid for probably contributed.* Denyse saw a WELCOME TO FORKS sign. "Should we have an early lunch here?"

Jeremy looked at Denyse again through the rearview. "What's available, sweetheart?"

"Pizza or burgers."

"What would you like, Miss Cossack?" asked Jeremy.

"Pizza."

"Okay. But I'm betting the pizzas here don't have garlic."

"According to you, maybe they should."

Jeremy laughed out loud. "We can have lunch here, visit the collection of Twilight props and costumes at the Rainforest Arts Center, take a walk in the woods like Bella, and then go to the rugged Washington coast. When I went fishing with Dad and Casey, I saw waves crashing on rocks similar to south Australia and mounds of driftwood, including tremendous whole trees."

* * *

Upstairs at the ranch house, Katie listened while Wilma poured out a litany of abuses. "It wasn't a real marriage of two people. I was a woman owned by a man. I had no rights at all. A virtual prisoner and slave."

Wilma sipped coffee occasionally while she and Katie cared for the three children. "I should have known better. But at only eighteen and having never really been off the farm, who would? Clyde, as he was named then, seemed so strong and confident. Men looked up to him. Now I'm ready for a new life. I just want to take my kids somewhere we can live life rather than endure it."

A middle-aged woman who had just arrived entered the kitchen. "I'm from Family Services in Wenatchee, here to take the children."

"Oh, please don't," pleaded Wilma. "They're all I have." She broke down sobbing.

"Could we talk a minute?" Katie asked the services representative. Once they were apart, she explained, "This woman has been through a lot. The children need their mother—"

The woman broke in. "Are you a state officer?"

"No, I—"

Aaron's voice interrupted Katie. "Ms. Stansky is fully cooperating with the state. And she's a potential witness to a criminal enterprise. I don't think separating the children from her is in anybody's best interest right now."

"But state rules clearly require that when abuse is suspected, the children must be removed."

"Ms. Stansky has been the one abused. A women's shelter is more appropriate," argued Katie.

"That hasn't been proven."

Katie spoke sternly, "This woman is distraught and traumatized. Separate her from her children and she could commit suicide."

Aaron directly addressed the service representative. "Does Family Services want to take that risk?"

One of the FBI agents heard the discussion and intervened. "Ms. Stansky is considered a candidate for witness protection. We can hold her and the children in an undisclosed hotel."

"Can everybody accept that?" asked Katie.

Nods and murmurs all around indicated agreement. Katie returned to Wilma. "You and the children will be taken together to a hotel under FBI protection. You should pack some bags. The authorities will sort this all out. But you'll stay together."

Wilma hugged Katie as Aaron approached. "Ms. Stansky, the records you revealed indicate that Mr. Jackson may have hidden some valuables nearby. Would you have any idea where that hiding place might be?"

"I don't know. But I sometimes saw him digging in an unusual spot."

"Before you leave, would you show us that spot?"

"Yes, I will."

* * *

"Your honor, the DA's office does not think a new trial for Anton Stegall is warranted even if his attorneys claim judicial bias." Bethany glanced at the table where Stegall sat with two highly paid attorneys from a major law firm. "A jury of Americans, not the trial judge, handed down the guilty verdict based on the evidence. Moreover, how can the defense possibly claim judicial bias? The court records will show that during cross-examination of Seattle's key witness, I objected to the questioning several times. In every instance, Judge Harmon ruled for the defense."

"Thank you, Ms. Turner," said the appeals court judge. "I'll review everything and make a ruling in a few weeks."

* * *

Two days after the "ranch raid," as Katie had dubbed the search warrants and arrest of Andrew Jackson, Dave and Katie were still recuperating from exhaustion in their hotel room. Katie's phone buzzed and indicated Aaron as the caller. Katie held the phone where Dave could see. "Should I answer?"

Dave sighed from exhaustion but held his hand out for the phone. "Hello, Aaron." Dave switched to speaker so Katie could participate.

Without pleasantries, Aaron reported, "We arrested Boone and his wife then searched his house. Didn't find anything new except some rifles illegally altered to be fully automatic. They both demanded a lawyer but won't communicate even with their public defenders.

"Unfortunately, the two militiamen ranch hands Ms. Stansky reported to be in the barn got away. We found two horses missing. They must have put the word out because most other militiamen on the list haven't been located.

"The dig spot Jackson's wife showed us yielded two hundred eighty-one thousand dollars in cash. By civil forfeiture, DFW and the state police will share that and the offshore money when recovered. We'll need it to pursue the multitude of leads you found in the records. Thank you, Katie, for befriending Wilma Stansky. I don't think she would have remained cooperative if we had separated her from her kids."

"You're welcome," responded Katie. "How are Wilma and her kids doing at the hotel?"

"My FBI contact says the Stanskys are having a grand time staying in the hotel and ordering delivery food. The maid service has helped Wilma to relax. She's providing a lot of inside information to the FBI, especially about heavily armed anti-government militias. The two older kids are loving the hotel's swimming pool and streaming Disney+ on the TV."

"What's next for the Stanskys?"

"Ms. Stansky is trying to decide between witness protection or just going home to her parents' farm in Oregon. Either way, they'll regret leaving the hotel."

Dave and Katie couldn't help laughing. "Sounds like we've done our part," said Dave. "Can we go home now?"

"Almost. Could you wait until after the initial arraignments in case we need you?"

"Of course."

"One thing still bothers me, though," Aaron continued. "We didn't find anything solid about Hal Dulfer's disappearance. All we have is an excited utterance Katie remembers. Based on that, I feel certain Boone and Jackson are involved somehow. But the utterance would be useless in a court.”

Dave sensed Aaron’s frustration. “I’ve got an idea. Have you arrested Brian Manning?”

“You mean Boone’s associate, Buddy? No, we haven’t. He’s low level. All we can really prove is him feeding bears.”

“He hasn’t changed his name like the militia stalwarts. And I couldn’t find his name in Jackson’s list of militiamen. Boone says he’s not smart. I doubt he’s an official member of the militia. He just does heavy work for Boone. This is a longshot, but let me and Katie go talk with him. Maybe we’ll learn something.”

“Okay. I’d need to go along and provide protection for you.”

“I was hoping you’d say that.”

Chapter Twenty-two

Katie sat in the back seat of their rental SUV giving directions from her phone to the outskirts of Shelton. "Buddy lives in the next house."

Dave parked in the driveway of a dilapidated wooden house behind the older white pickup they associated with Buddy.

"Buddy must be home. That's his truck," Katie told Aaron, who sat in the van's passenger seat next to Dave.

"You'll do most of the talking, like we agreed," Aaron said to Dave.

"Right."

The three opened the SUV's doors and got out. Aaron followed Dave and Katie to the front door. An unkempt older woman answered Dave's knock. "We're looking for Buddy," Dave said.

The woman turned her head and shouted, "Buddy, you got visitors." She then disappeared, leaving the door open.

Katie heard a grunt from inside, then Buddy came. His large frame seemed to fill the door.

"We're friends of Willis Boone, Buddy," Dave explained. "You've seen me and my wife, Katie, with Willis at the gun shop. He took us bear hunting."

Buddy nodded. "Yeah."

"We have some money for Willis but can't find him. We thought you could help us."

"Maybe."

Dave gestured at Aaron, who stood wearing fatigues with a Pioneer Spirit patch prominently displayed and a sidearm. "Come on out and meet Davy Crockett, another friend of Willis's."

Aaron extended a hand to shake. Buddy stepped outside to take the proffered hand. After shaking, Aaron pointed to the Pioneer Spirit patch Buddy wore. "Always glad to meet a teammate."

Buddy smiled, revealing chewing-tobacco-stained teeth. "Yeah."

"Buddy here works for Willis. He carries the heavy loads Willis can't. Buddy knows how to keep his mouth shut around stinking government agents. You can trust him, Davy."

"How can I be sure Buddy is trustworthy?" asked Aaron.

Dave turned to Buddy. "Crockett is the suspicious type. Tell him the biggest secret you've kept for Willis."

Katie held her breath.

But Buddy appeared eager to be trusted. "I've helped skin bears out of hunting season and packed the pelts out at night."

Aaron shook his head. "We've all done that."

"Come on, Buddy. Help Crockett trust you with something *big*," urged Dave.

"I carried a body for him once. A man Willis had to kill in self-defense. We buried the body together."

Katie saw Aaron clench his teeth while forcing an appreciative smile.

Dave smiled himself and joshed Buddy. "You did not! Why would anyone want to kill Willis?"

"I did too. He was a stinking government agent. All Willis did was shoot a bear on the Sol Duc."

"How do you know the would-be killer was a government agent?"

"He wore a uniform. Willis took his badge and his gun."

"Did you see the killing happen?"

"No, Willis called my mother and asked her to send me to help and to bring a shovel. When I got there, Willis told me the agent had tried to kill him. I dug a hole in the forest and buried the body."

"When was this?"

"'Bout a year ago. The salmon were running."

"Where did you dig the hole?"

Buddy shrugged. "Away from the river. Somewhere back in the forest. I can't remember exactly where."

"How far from the river?"

Buddy pointed at a tree about a hundred and fifty feet away. "'Bout as far as that tree."

"Was there a car involved?"

"Yeah. Willis drove it to a junkyard while I followed in my pickup. The militiamen there laughed when they saw a government car. Then I drove Willis back to pick up his truck. Willis gave me five hundred dollars for helping."

Dave turned to Aaron. "See? I told you Buddy here could be trusted."

Aaron shrugged. "I guess you were right. Buddy is a true teammate." He paused before adding, "I sure would like to see that badge, though. Do you know what Willis did with that badge, Buddy? Then we would know for sure that you're one of us."

"Willis called the badge 'the ultimate trophy' and sold it. A man came at night to collect it. Willis called him Captain. I got another five hundred dollars from him."

Dave looked at Aaron, who nodded. "Thank you, Buddy. You've helped us a lot. I'm sure Davy Crockett here will want to talk to you some more another time." Dave and Aaron shook hands with Buddy and turned to go. Katie followed them back to the SUV.

As Dave drove away, Katie asked Aaron, "Why didn't you arrest Buddy? He's guilty of accessory to murder after the fact at the very least."

Aaron shook his head. "Did you see how big he is? We'd need a squad of men to bring him in."

Dave laughed. "Maybe even a tranquilizer gun."

Aaron joined Dave chuckling. "Buddy's not going anywhere. We might learn more from him later."

* * *

Aaron used a microphone to address a score of DFW officers and Forest Service rangers, three police officers with cadaver dogs, and a mixed group of two hundred volunteers Casey had recruited through his blog. Jeremy, Denyse, and Sandra joined the volunteers. Several reporters had arrived to cover the search. A state forensics team stood by.

"We believe Hal Dulfer's body is buried in a forest area maybe a hundred to two hundred feet away from the river. Look for anything unusual—a depression, undergrowth, evidence of digging by scavengers. If you suspect a spot, don't dig yourself but phone me. I'll send an officer with a cadaver dog."

Seven hours and many unfruitful reports later, one of Casey's young women volunteers called Aaron for the second time. "The canine officer you sent asked me to call. He says his dog is positive about this spot."

"Thanks! I'll send the forensics team."

An hour later Aaron called in the searchers by text alert. *Body found. Reassemble at the start point.*

Once the searchers had reassembled, they waited while drinking water and soft drinks provided by DFW. Aaron spoke to them again. "I'd like to thank all of you for helping us, especially my fellow followers of Washington Coalition for Sustainability." He pointed out the young woman who had located the spot. After waiting for polite applause to fade, Aaron added, "This is Casey Carpenter, to whom you responded. Casey played a major role in solving this case as well as the animal trafficking ring you've seen in the news."

Casey took the microphone. "This is a sad day. A man dedicated to the environment and sustainability lost his life in that effort. We have a disparate group here. You are environmentalists, hunters, fishermen, conservationists, hikers, birdwatchers, scientists, and outdoors lovers of all kinds. We all share Hal Dulfer's commitment to protect and sustain our world." Longer and louder applause answered him. "Please allow me to introduce someone else who initiated the investigation that resulted in solving this crime." Casey pointed at Bethany. "This is Bethany Turner, my fiancée." More applause followed. Reporters converged on Bethany.

"Come look at this," Jeremy called to Denyse from in front of the hotel room TV.

Denyse came in carrying freshly bathed David wrapped in a towel. "What is it?"

"The Pioneer Spirit Militia has taken over the courthouse in Olympia."

The TV screen showed a heavily armed mob of about a hundred men and a few women standing behind a spokesman. Police officers watched and listened from a distance. "This building is on publicly owned land. As American citizens, we own this land and have the right to be here."

"Why *are* you here?" asked a local reporter holding the microphone.

"We're here in support of our captain who has been unlawfully arrested for exercising his constitutional right to bear arms and utilize public lands. Release Andrew Jackson and we'll leave."

The reporter stepped away and faced the camera. "So far there has been no violence. Olympia police are standing down and keeping the public away, hoping to deescalate a potentially dangerous situation. This is KATY TV reporting live from the state court at the James M. Dolliver Building in Olympia. Back to you, Tom and Ethyl."

The picture changed to show two anchors of a local TV station on set. Tom looked into the studio camera. "Arraignment of Andrew Jackson on multiple charges of poaching and animal trafficking had been scheduled for later today. The governor has just made a statement."

A clip showed Washington's governor at the capitol speaking in front of a microphone and flanked by various officials, including Director Hodgekiss of DFW. "This is an armed insurrection. I've just issued orders to call out our national guard."

Jeremy and Denyse looked at each other. "Weren't Dave and Katie supposed to testify at

Andrew Jackson's arraignment in Olympia?" asked
Denyse.

Chapter Twenty-three

Dave and Katie stood with Aaron behind the line of local and state police surrounding the courthouse and keeping curiosity seekers at bay. "Doesn't look like the arraignment will proceed today," said Dave.

Aaron's phone buzzed. He placed it to his ear and listened. "Okay. Thanks!" He hung up and said, "Don't be too sure about Jackson's arraignment not occurring today. Judge Monroe is convening the state court at Olympia's municipal courthouse."

"Where's that?" asked Dave.

"Just a few blocks away. We can walk there. But authorities aren't publicizing the move, lest the militia crazies join us."

The first contingents of the national guard passed in army trucks as they walked. "What will the army do?" asked Katie.

Aaron answered, "I'm guessing the guard will seal off the area around the courthouse. Then allow the state police to try negotiating a surrender. In a way, this is a break for DFW. We'd have had a difficult time tracking down all the poachers and animal traffickers implicated in Jackson's records. Now the worst are located and contained."

"And heavily armed," interjected Dave.

Aaron's phone rang again. "This is Officer Wierzbowski. Uh-huh. Uh-huh. Thanks." Aaron swiped off. "That was the state crime lab. A bullet found in Hal Dulfer's body matches the 30-30 ballistics we already have. We've got Boone on murder now even without Buddy's testimony. I'd bet my pension that Jackson is involved too, at least as an accessory after the fact. We just need to prove it."

The Parkers waited for three hours until Dave was called before the court to explain his interpretation of the records located at Jackson's ranch. He repeated his preliminary conclusions, "This indicates the operation of a criminal enterprise led by Andrew Jackson."

Jackson's attorney stood up. "The defense objects to Mr. Parker's objectivity making this cursory report. He was apparently a part of the DFW investigation that led to the arrest of my client. Mr. Parker should recuse himself."

"This is an arraignment, not a trial," returned Judge Monroe. "Overruled."

Wilma Stansky arrived escorted by the FBI and testified to authenticate the records Dave had studied. She added fraudulent activities she had observed. Wilma smiled and waved at Katie as the FBI whisked her away afterwards.

On the question of bail, Judge Monroe cited Jackson's armed supporters holding the James M. Dolliver Building hostage. "Remanded without bail."

Outside the courtroom Aaron warned, "You two need to be careful. Some militiamen could blame you."

"I thought the national guard had them all penned up," returned Katie.

"There are probably some latecomers outside the perimeter."

After Aaron hurried away, Dave lingered, watching the legal wrangling. He thought about the trial of Anton Stegall that had brought his family to Washington state. *Where did Anton Stegall put the missing money?* he wondered. He thought about his arraignment testimony an hour earlier. *The log had one entry marked "AS" for a hundred thousand dollars. Quite a few AS entries, in fact. Could AS be Anton Stegall?*

As they walked to where they had parked the rental SUV, Dave told Katie about his suspicion.

Katie shook her head. "Isn't that coincidence unlikely?"

"Yes. But as Einstein said, 'Coincidence is God's way of remaining anonymous.'"

* * *

Bethany's buzzing phone indicated a call from Casey. Although sitting in a meeting, her heart warmed and she stepped out of the conference room. She justified her action: *I shouldn't refuse a call from my fiancée. I still can't get used to being engaged, though.* "Hello, Casey."

"I just got off the phone with Tara and Jeff. I've accepted the managerial job of their new outdoors store. I appreciate you letting me decide without pressure."

Bethany hid her relief. "What made you decide?"

"I couldn't see how we could start a family with your salary and meager funding from my nonprofit and . . ."

"And what else?" Bethany prompted.

"I once heard a story about a cathedral being built. A bishop visited the workers. He asked a dispirited-looking stonemason what he was doing.

'I'm chiseling this rock,' the man said. Nearby, another stonemason worked happily, humming to himself. The bishop asked the same question. 'I'm building a cathedral,' that man replied. Bethany, I won't just be managing a sporting goods store. I'll be building a movement."

Bethany looked back at the conference room where lawyers haggled about cases, priorities, and resources. *What am I building?*

* * *

KATY TV ran a special report with the headline, SUSPECTS ACCUSED OF CRIMINAL ENTERPRISE.

A reporter interviewed DFW Director Hodgekiss about the arrests, arraignments, and discovery of Hal Dulfer's body. "The investigation is ongoing, especially related to Officer Dulfer's murder," stated Hodgekiss. "Some individuals implicated by evidence are still holed up in the James M. Dolliver Building." The director introduced Aaron Wierzbowski as the detective leading the investigation.

Aaron led the reporter to tables on which he had displayed illicit trophies. "These are some items we confiscated at the Jackson ranch near Wenatchee."

"Is that an orca skin?" the reporter asked.

"Yes. And apparently orca meat was served at various meetings or drills at the Jackson ranch."

"At the discovery of Officer Dulfer's body, you credited private citizen Casey Carpenter as playing a major role in the investigation. Carpenter heads a nonprofit, the Washington Coalition for Sustainability."

"Yes, that is correct. DFW is grateful for Casey's help and for his blog followers who joined the search for Hal's body. One of those volunteers actually found the shallow grave."

"Mr. Carpenter also introduced Bethany Turner as being an instigator in this investigation. Ms. Turner is an assistant DA for Seattle. Isn't an assistant DA instigating an investigation on her own unusual?"

* * *

Bethany found an email from Seattle's DA on her computer. *Come to my office.*

This doesn't sound good, she thought.

With Bethany seated in front of his desk, the DA streamed a portion of KATY TV's special report. "Did you instigate a personal investigation?"

"Yes."

"In pursuing your unauthorized investigation, however worthy a cause, did you access police reports and use information on private citizens from the state's records?"

"I did," Bethany admitted.

The DA sighed. "I was afraid so. Bethany, you're very talented and dedicated. But we can't tolerate officers of the court mounting personal investigations and violating the privacy of private citizens. Even though your investigation revealed major crimes, I'm suspending you for a month without pay starting immediately. I hope you'll take your discipline then come back."

"Yes, sir."

Bethany felt humiliated while collecting her personal items. Others in the DA's office didn't make eye contact as she departed. Once outside the building, she acknowledged to herself, *He didn't fire me. The punishment is lenient. I knew better.* Then she realized, *This will be an indelible stain on my record. Fortunately, I've saved several months of salary for an emergency. I guess this qualifies.*

Thoughts of the indictments buoyed her spirits. *It was worth it.* She remembered Casey's excitement about building a sustainability movement and a business. *What am I building?* she asked herself again.

Bethany sat down on a bench and dialed Casey.

"This is an unusual time for you to call," said Casey when answering.

"You got me suspended!" Before Casey could respond she added, "It wasn't your fault, though."

"Specifically what did I do?" he asked.

"In front of TV cameras, you gave me credit for starting the investigation. That's how the DA found out. But how can I be angry at a non-lawyer like you for praising me in public?"

"Sorry. I think you're terrific. Can't help praising you."

"I'm looking forward to getting used to that."

"So now what do you think about starting your own practice?" asked Casey. "I can give you plenty of clients and free office space immediately."

* * *

Sandra stared out the hotel window down at the parking lot while the children slept. Denyse and Jeremy had gone to give formal statements to DFW about the forest stakeout. They would also provide details of the delivery of the raccoon and bear cub to animal rescue. She heard Dave and Katie leave their room and head downstairs on their way to be deposed by the state police in their part of the search and arrests at Jackson's ranch.

From her third-floor vantage point, Sandra saw a man concealing himself behind a white windowless van with an open sliding door. She heard the hotel's first-floor door open and Dave's voice joking about something. The man pulled an AR-15-style rifle from the van and pointed it toward the hotel door. Sandra gasped and picked up a lamp, then used it to break the window's glass. "Gunman! Gunman!" she screamed as Dave and Katie entered the parking lot.

The gunman involuntarily looked up at her shouting. In that instant, Dave pushed Katie to the pavement behind a parked car and lay on her. Bullets fired on automatic smashed the glass doors behind where Dave and Katie had stood only seconds earlier then shifted to riddle the car where they had taken refuge.

The gunman paused to change the bullet clip. Sandra kept screaming warnings through the window she had broken. She saw the gunman look up and point the automatic rifle at her. Sandra dove to the floor and started crawling to where the children slept. A dozen bullets smashed through the window. The noise of the gun fired in her direction seemed deafening. She grabbed each of the children by one hand and dragged them forcibly into the hotel room's bathroom.

Chapter Twenty-four

Dave and Katie crawled along the line of parked cars while the shooter fired at Sandra. After changing the bullet clip again, the gunman stalked to where Dave and Katie had originally dived but found nobody. Cursing, the shooter returned to the van, threw the rifle inside, closed the sliding door, and started the engine. Hearing an engine start, Katie peeked over the car serving as their current hiding place. She saw a white van leaving and quickly memorized the Nevada license tag number.

Dave rose to his feet and looked up at the shattered window of Jeremy and Denyse's room. "Are you okay, Katie?" he shouted.

Katie saw blood on the ground. It streamed from her scraped knee where Dave had thrown her down. "I'm alright. Go check on our grandchildren."

Dave stepped through the shattered hotel door and disappeared inside. Sirens sounded in the distance as Katie followed Dave. Upstairs she found

David and Katelyn frightened and crying from having been dragged into the bathroom. Sandra was hysterically screaming "Poppa! Poppa! Poppa!" and clutching Dave around his waist.

"I found Sandra lying on top of the children in the shower stall," Dave told her. "When she saw me, she went crazy. David and Katelyn appear frightened but are otherwise okay."

Sandra released Dave and clutched Katie. "Mama, Mama."

Katie spoke quietly to Dave over Sandra's shoulder. "I'm not a psychologist but I did teach teenagers for many years. I believe Sandra has suppressed her grief from the death of her father due to the trauma their family experienced afterwards. She sees us as parental figures and is flashing back to unimaginable horror."

Katie tilted her head toward David and Katelyn. "Take them to our room and comfort them." Then Katie turned her attention to Sandra, hugging her and saying, "We're all safe, honey. You saved us."

Police appeared at the door with drawn weapons. "Where is the gunman?" one asked.

"Escaped in a white van with a Nevada license tag." Katie recited the tag number.

"Anyone hurt here?" another officer asked.

"We're only shaken up."

"Gunman fleeing in a white van," The first officer reported into his radio and gave the state and tag number.

Sandra released Katie and sat on the bed quietly weeping. *All this girl has experienced is catching up to her,* realized Katie. She sat beside Sandra. "Cry all you want, honey. You're due."

Sandra sobbed. "I couldn't save my Poppa in Ukraine. I couldn't keep our family together."

"You saved Dave and me, though. And perhaps David and Katelyn. You're a heroine, honey."

Two hours later Aaron arrived at the Baymont hotel after being called by Dave. He found Denyse and Sandra fussing over the happy children in Dave and Katie's room, Jeremy moving possessions from the damaged room to another in the hotel, and Dave and Katie congratulating Bethany and Casey on their engagement.

Dave called them all together. "Obviously, our investigation isn't finished."

"You mean because Jackson's militia tried to assassinate you and Mom," suggested Jeremy.

"I'm not sure about that. Aaron, is there any news about the gunman?"

"He strikes me as being more of a thug than a professional hitman. A toll collector for the Tacoma Narrows Bridge reported him headed south on

Highway 16. Tacoma's police identified him on I-5 south. The state patrol set up a trap and arrested a white male named Gerald Rubin in a van bearing the Nevada license tag Katie reported. They recovered a weapon he likely used. He isn't cooperating. The state police found a woman's name and address inside the van."

"Is the address a condo in Las Vegas?"

"How did you know that?" Aaron wanted to know.

"I'm guessing based on a series of coincidences. First, the biggest customer for illicit trophies in Jackson's logbook is designated by 'AS,' which could stand for Anton Stegall." Dave heard Bethany gasp but continued, "My search for Stegall's assets revealed a condo in Las Vegas. Bethany, is there any reason Stegall would want me dead?"

"Well, vengeance, of course. More importantly, Stegall's lawyers have requested a retrial. If you weren't available to testify at a retrial, a conviction would be unlikely."

Dave continued, "The gunman might have been targeting just me. And that gunman came from . . ."

"Nevada," finished Denyse.

Dave nodded. "Right. I never accounted for all the money Stegall swindled. But I didn't think to have the condo in Las Vegas physically searched.

Some of the missing assets could be there in the form of trophies. Finally, a woman at the end of Stegall's trial gave me the most hateful look. A woman's name was found in the gunman's van associated with the condo. We might find her living there. Maybe as Stegall's mistress. If so, she probably wouldn't have access to professional hitmen. Would just hire a thug."

The group remained silent after Dave's recitation of connections. "We need to search that condo," said Aaron.

"Yes, we do," responded Dave. "Bethany, can you help us get a search warrant in Las Vegas?"

Bethany didn't answer for a long moment while everybody waited. She made eye contact with Casey, who nodded for her to go ahead. "I've been suspended from the Seattle DA's office. I launched an independent investigation and accessed private records, violating ethics standards."

Everybody verbalized condolences. Sandra surprised all by asking Bethany, "What will you do now?"

"I can return to the DA's office after a month. But that black mark on my record would handicap my future career. For now, I'm going to help Casey open a store in Olympia. He's offered me office space for a legal practice. Maybe I can represent causes Casey and I believe in."

"Tara will come here starting next week to receive ordered merchandise, direct the store's setup, and coach me as the manager," Casey explained.

Questions and congratulations came for a long time until Dave broke in, "We're all truly happy for you. Now what about a search warrant in Las Vegas?"

"I can contact our fish and wildlife counterparts in Nevada. They can help us contact the correct authorities and get a warrant to be executed by Las Vegas police," offered Aaron.

* * *

Aaron waited while Las Vegas police officers knocked on the door of an exclusive high-rise condo and served a search warrant to the woman who answered. He entered after the police verified the absence of danger. Immediately he saw displays with illicit trophies and orca-hide carpets. In the most prominent spot, Hal Dulfer's badge and gun had been displayed and labeled THE ULTIMATE TROPHY along with a photo of Jackson and Stegall together.

"That stuff isn't mine," the woman insisted. "I only live here for free rent."

Aaron saw the woman's phone lying on a coffee table. He picked it up and scrolled through the phone numbers. First he found Andrew Jackson with a record of texts. Scrolling a little further, Gerald Rubin's number—the gunman who had shot at Dave and Katie—appeared. "Arrest her for attempted murder and read her the rights," he told the police officers.

"I'll cooperate for a deal," the handcuffed woman offered. "I can testify against Anton Stegall."

One policeman came to Aaron with a cardboard box full of hundred-dollar bills. "What shall I do with this?"

Aaron shrugged. "It could belong to the Las Vegas Police Department by civil forfeiture. Or it could revert to Anton Stegall's defrauded investors. Lawyers and judges will have to decide. For now, I'd put it into a sealed evidence bag. We can all sign to document the finding."

Aaron opened the camera bag he carried and started taking pictures.

At 6:00 a.m., Katie watched while Jeremy and Denyse checked in at SeaTac Airport, no small task with two young children. Dave stood by holding a bag for Sandra, who was waiting to take a later flight to Melbourne. Sandra appeared sad.

Their bags checked in and boarding passes printed, Denyse approached and hugged Sandra. "I know you agreed to care for David and Katelyn in return for an expense-paid trip to America, but Jeremy and I wanted to express how grateful we are." Denyse handed her five hundred-dollar bills.

Sandra's voice revealed her struggle to maintain self-control. "Thank you." Then she spoke to Jeremy, "Good luck in the election this fall. You'll make a great senator."

"Thank you, Sandra. Deciding to run for office has been difficult," Jeremy responded before changing the conversation's direction. "I've really enjoyed having a younger sister."

Denyse gently pushed her children forward. "Say goodbye to Aunt Sandra. Give her a final hug."

Katelyn turned her eyes to her mother. "We won't see Sandra again?"

"Maybe not for a long time."

Sandra reached out and hugged Katelyn. "I love you."

Katelyn started to cry. "I love you too, Aunt Sandra." David didn't understand goodbyes but cried in sympathy with his older sister. Tears ran down Sandra's cheeks as she hugged David.

Dave interrupted, surprising them all. "Katie and I are going to drive across the country starting with the Oregon Trail, Sandra. Why don't you go to the ticket counter and postpone your return to Melbourne? You can ride with us across America."

Sandra's face lit up. "Do you really mean it?"

"You never know when we might need saving again," Dave quipped.

Katie thought, *Dave should really consult with me before making such invitations. But in this case, he's a genius.* "Yes, honey. We would love your company. With Dave you'll mostly see historic sites and museums. Maybe a few parks. The journey will also take us to nice hotels, cute towns, restaurants, and shopping. You and I will have a good time together."

Sandra looked at Denyse, who nodded vigorously in support. "Thank you, I would love that."

Katie thought, *If Dave can make unilateral invitations, so can I.* "Afterwards you can stay with us as long as you choose, honey. But because we're old-fashioned there will be rules. And you'll need to pitch in on housework."

"Of course, I will."

Dave joined Katie's offer. "Stay into fall and you could take courses at the University of South Alabama in Mobile. You're good at math, I'm told. You could earn some money by working part time at our accounting firm. Or Denyse would gladly pay you rather than the child-care center while she teaches."

"But there are no vampires in Alabama," teased Jeremy. "You will get to go fishing and crabbing with us. But you'll need to learn the words 'War Eagle.'"

"Okay. What does War Eagle mean?"

Denyse sighed. "That's support for the Parkers' favorite American football team."

"American football?" Sandra questioned.

"That's a lullaby of violence Dave sleeps to in front of our TV," explained Katie.

"You'll see Aunt Sandra again very soon," Denyse reassured Katelyn and David. Then she looked at Jeremy. "We should get through security."

Katie, along with Dave and Sandra, waited until the younger Parkers disappeared. A familiar female voice surprised her. "Did we miss Jeremy and Denyse? There was an accident that slowed traffic on I-5 to a crawl." Bethany and Casey had come to say goodbye along with Aaron.

Katie noticed that Bethany wore a diamond engagement ring. "Sorry. They just went through security."

"Phone them, Bethany," urged Casey.

Bethany and Casey stepped away to call Jeremy and Denyse. Aaron remained with the Parkers and Sandra.

"Nice work down in Las Vegas, Aaron," said Dave. "How's the militia and national guard standoff going?"

Aaron laughed. "It's about over. Deserters have been surrendering for days. Most had jobs they wanted to keep. Being a weekend revolutionary can give a rush but doesn't pay the bills. Some missed their wives and children. I also think all of them were worried about leaving their pickup trucks unattended and vulnerable to thieves in Olympia."

"What are you doing with the deserters?"

"We have a list of those implicated by the records you examined. We'll arrest them. They'll see that courthouse again. A few are already asking for plea bargains in exchange for cooperation. Those on whom we have nothing serious—and we don't count being a sucker as serious—we'll ticket for trespassing. We know where to find them if evidence of more serious crimes surfaces.

"By the way, we used Jackson's records to trace and recover black bear forty-two's male bear cub, the brother of the female Katie rescued. The wildlife rehabilitation center has both cubs now. Northwest Trek Wildlife Park in Pierce County has offered to take them once they've been weaned."

"That's good news," said Katie. "Denyse will be glad to hear that."

"Thanks again for reimbursing us for the moneys we gave to Boone during the stings," said Dave.

"The right thing to do. And it came out of the money you helped us locate."

Bethany and Casey returned. "We told Jeremy and Denyse you had come," Casey told Aaron. "They praised you for a tremendous job and invited you and your family to visit Mobile."

"Every one of you did a tremendous job," said Dave.

"And you too," added Katie.

Dave smiled at his wife. "Thank you, sweetheart." Then looking at the others, he said, "Let me treat us all to breakfast. Then Katie and I along with Sandra will hit the trail. That is, the Oregon Trail."

Aaron shook his head. "Sorry, I've got to finish up organizing DFW's participation in Hal's funeral. I also need to pack our car for a two-week camping trip to California and Disneyland with my wife and kids. We'll leave soon after the funeral."

Dave looked at Bethany and Casey. "Aaron's driving," said Casey. "But I'm expecting Tara and Jeff to arrive with their kids today, anyway. Shipments of merchandise are waiting for unpacking and display."

"I've got client meetings scheduled with potential plaintiffs," Bethany added. "And I want to help Casey at Outdoors Always. Thanks for the offer, though."

"I'm ready to head east if you are, Sandra," said Katie. "We can get breakfast on the road."

"Let us get started then," Sandra answered.

* * *

A week later Dave, Katie, and Sandra sat in the Old Faithful Inn dining room in Yellowstone National Park. "Didn't I promise you that we'd have some fun on Dave's trip, Sandra?" said Katie.

Sandra looked around at the cavernous space below a ceiling of natural wood supported by a truss of peeled logs. She saw a massive stone fireplace at one end of the restaurant. "More fun than I could have imagined," she answered.

"Same with me," Dave added. "One wagon rut in Idaho looks pretty much like all the other ruts." Dave looked appreciatively at Katie. "I'm glad you insisted we detour to Wyoming's parks."

"So we're finished with the Oregon Trail?" asked Sandra.

"No, but the route gets more interesting. After this we'll go over South Pass where most of the pioneers crossed the continental divide. Without that break in the Rocky Mountains, American settlers probably couldn't have flooded into the northwest. What we know of as Washington, Oregon, and northern California could have been British or maybe even Russian."

"Russian?"

"Sure. Russia had plenty of settlements in what is now Alaska." Dave paused before continuing, "After South Pass we'll follow the North Platte River and in Nebraska see famous landmarks along the trail like Chimney Rock."

Katie knew that once started Dave could drone on about historical minutia. "I'm going to try the bison burger," she said while looking at the menu. "They offer cornbread muffins. Do you think their cornbread is like our Southern cornbread or sweetened?"

"I'd guess sweetened," answered Dave.

"If you don't like their recipe, I could eat the muffins," said Sandra. "In Ukraine, most cornbreads include sugar. Sweet cornbread muffins could go well with the bison bratwurst. My Poppa used to make bratwurst. I haven't had any since leaving Ukraine."

"You might be disappointed with American bratwurst, honey. But you should try it. Then when we get to Mobile, I'll make you some Southern cornbread," teased Katie.

"Ladies, get whatever you might like," interjected Dave. "I'll eat anything that you don't."

Katie's phone buzzed with a text. "Oh, it's from Casey. I've been wondering if there are any new developments in Washington. He sent some video links to my email." She opened her email and tapped the first link. First she smiled, then she laughed. "This is Tara being interviewed on a local TV station. Casey had credited her as an instigator of the investigation."

"What's so funny about that?" asked Dave.

"Tara manages to use the interview as a plug for the opening of Outdoors Always, their outdoor supply store in Olympia. She's even standing where the camera picks up the store front and emblem."

Dave smiled. "I'm not surprised."

"Listen, Dave. When Tara goes public with her company—and she will eventually—I want you to invest all our savings in her stock. We'll become famously rich."

"I wouldn't put all our savings in any one investment."

"Well, a lot then."

Katie tapped another link on Casey's email. "The other link is the local news covering Hal's funeral. There's Aaron escorting Hal's wife and children in between lines of uniformed DFW officers to bagpipe music. The clip then shows Washington's governor eulogizing Hal. The reporter goes on to say that a wildlife refuge is being renamed to honor Hal."

Katie shut down her phone. "I'll run the clips on my laptop tonight for you and Sandra to watch. Casey also wrote that Bethany has moved to Olympia and is swamped with new clients."

"If I could invest in a law firm, I'd like to put some money there too," said Dave.

"You've got that right."

Sandra watched Dave and Katie interacting and prayed, *Dear God, please let me have a marriage like this.*

Then she volunteered, "Thank you for telling me stories about your lives as we ride. You have had great adventures together."

Katie laughed. "We've enjoyed hearing about your life in Ukraine too. Adventures aren't always fun at the time. But afterwards, especially as you get older, they can be great fun to remember."

Epilogue

On Christmas Eve, Katie logged into a Zoom meeting from her living room and watched faces appear on her laptop screen. Dave joined from his home office and Sandra logged on using her cellphone from a recliner near Katie. Jeremy and Denyse with their children joined from Denyse's computer at home on their couch. Logging in from Australia, Katie saw Sandra's sisters Sveta and Lena, along with Lena's husband and Denyse's brother, Trevor, plus Denyse's parents, Dingo and Beatrice.

Sandra could not wait to talk. "I met a guy. Oleksiy is the born-in-America son of Ukrainian immigrants. He was one of Denyse's calculus students who came to thank her for helping him qualify for engineering school. He first invited me to a movie. After that I went with him to what they call 'homecoming' at Auburn. We attended a big, noisy, American football game. I stayed with very nice girls in their dormitory. Oleksiy has lots of American friends who are very dedicated to God. We went everywhere together. Several girls told me what a good man Oleksiy is. I even learned to shout, 'War Eagle.' It was so exciting."

Katie wondered, *Is this the same timid girl we met in Washington just last July?* She prayed a short prayer knowing what Sandra intended to ask. Unlike Sandra, Katie knew that Denyse had already called her parents and had a long talk with them.

Sandra addressed Dingo and Beatrice. "Mama and Poppa, you have been very generous helping me go to the university in Melbourne. Auburn has a very good engineering school. Could I use that same money to attend Auburn? It is not enough, but Dave and Katie have offered to pay the difference. I promise to keep good grades and make you proud."

Beatrice had prepared their answer. "Yes, we will, luv. And we are already proud of you. We love all of you from Ukraine. Lena has made us into a family."

Dingo chimed in, "Yeah. Being in America has been good for you, Sandra. You even look different. Lass, you've become a stunner. And blimey, I never thought I would share a family with an engineer. Could give me the big head. Let me meet Oleksiy before you get serious, though. I'll be able to tell what sort of bloke he is."

"Thank you so much," Sandra said through her tears.

After Sandra quietened, those in Australia congratulated Jeremy for winning the election. "Which party are you?" asked Dingo.

"I ran as an independent," answered Jeremy.

"His campaign slogan was, 'Vote for sanity with careful decision-making'," volunteered Denyse.

Then Trevor asked about their adventure in Washington.

Dave summarized, "Aaron, the Washington law enforcement officer we worked with, reports that the poaching and animal trafficking criminal enterprise has been dismantled. A man named Boone will be tried for first-degree murder. The ringleader, Jackson, bartered his testimony against his clients and militia members for a twenty-year sentence. The anti-government Pioneer Spirit Militia disbanded after their captain turned on them to serve himself. Thirteen militia members received sentences of two to five years plus fines for poaching and animal trafficking. Fifty-three militia members paid fines of up to ten thousand dollars. Anton Stegall got life for fraud and has yet to face charges for attempted murder."

"Our murder," Katie interjected. "Sandra saved us and could have been shot herself."

"Good on ya, lass," Dingo responded. "You've got some Ned Kelly in ya."

"Wasn't there another couple who helped?" asked Lena.

"That was Bethany and Casey," answered Denyse. "They opened a very successful outdoor adventure store with an old girlfriend of Jeremy's."

To answer raised eyebrows in Australia, Denyse added, "An old girlfriend who helped Dave and Katie break up a drug-dealing ring. We all flew to Washington in November for Bethany and Casey's wedding. I never saw so much rain as Washington in November. Bethany has started her own law practice and is swamped with needy clients and causes."

The Zoom conversation continued for another hour as each family member shared their experiences. Afterward, Sandra joined Katie in the kitchen preparing for the Parker family traditional Cajun Christmas Eve dinner. When Denyse, Jeremy, and the kids arrived, Denyse joined Katie and Sandra in the kitchen while Jeremy took Katelyn and David to help their grandfather laying the wood for a Cajun bonfire to welcome Santa.

After dinner featuring Cajun jambalaya and the bonfire, Sandra went home with Jeremy and Denyse to experience early Christmas morning with the children receiving Santa's gifts. Afterwards she would help Denyse prepare Christmas dinner American/Australian/Ukrainian, for everyone.

Dave helped Katie clean up everything after the Cajun meal. "With all their responsibilities, I can't see how Bethany and Casey will find time for each other," he commented.

"They'll find moments for each other," predicted Katie.

"And eventually they'll slow down."

"Really? So when are you and I going to slow down?"

The Authors

Kit and Drew Coons met while living in Africa doing humanitarian work. There Kit taught in a teachers college while Drew worked to provide clean water to nineteen cities and towns.

As humorous speakers specializing in strengthening relationships, they have taught in every part of the US and in thirty-nine other countries. For two years, the Coonses lived and taught in New Zealand and Australia. They speak and write as a team.

Drew received honors degrees in engineering from both Auburn and Georgia Tech. He worked on the Delta Rocket program and designed critical components for the Space Shuttle. Later he served as a researcher for BASF Corporation and received twenty-three US and several international patents.

Kit has an honors degree in education from the University of Minnesota. She is a gifted teacher and blogger with an undaunted spirit regardless of the circumstances.

The Coonses are also the authors of many published articles and eight novels. The theme of their writing and website is **More Than Ordinary Lives**. They relocated to Port Orchard, Washington, in 2020.

What is a
more than ordinary life?

Each person's life is unique and special. In that sense, there is no such thing as an ordinary life. However, many people yearn for lives more special: excitement, adventure, romance, purpose, character. Not everyone can have the opportunities of a professional athlete, astronaut, movie star, or other celebrity.

 Then how can the rest of us lead more-than-ordinary lives? Our novels and website are dedicated to the premise that any life can be more than ordinary. We will post ideas and resources including inspiring stories about people enhancing their lives.

https://morethanordinarylives.com

Other Books by Kit and Drew Coons

Challenge Series of Mystery–Destination Novels with Dave and Katie

If Hallmark Mysteries joined Travel Channel

Dave and Katie Parker are an early-60s-aged couple forced into premature retirement and recovering from difficult circumstances. "I feel like our old life was a boat that went over a waterfall with us inside. Now we're bobbing up in the pool below, glad to be alive, but without a boat," says Katie.

The *Challenge Series* of novels follow the Parkers as they solve mysteries and find new adventures. Dave and Katie's relationship and ability to work as a team is deepened by each fish-out-of-water experience. They meet and help many colorful characters in charming settings. The situations frequently require the Parkers to face difficult choices and undergo personal growth. Readers will experience new places and cultures with Dave and Katie.

Admirable characters in each story and some redemptive themes make the stories meaningful. All the *Challenge* novels have been professionally illustrated.

Please see the Coonses' website for descriptions of each *Challenge Series* novel.

https://morethanordinarylives.com

Praise from readers about the *Challenge Series:*

"Have just finished your books and wanted to say thanks for great reads. A friend lent me your books while we are on virus hiatus. Keep writing, and I'll keep reading!" Susan - a retired librarian

"Hello Kit and Drew ! I received your Challenge series for Christmas, and I absolutely loved them. I was wondering if Dave and Katie are planning any new adventures. I just love their story! You two are wonderful. Thank you for sharing." Goodreads Review

"I don't know if you remember me, but I am the kid from Russellville. I love them so much. I was accepted into a national youth leadership forum, and I was interviewed by the Courier newspaper here in Russellville. I mentioned your book series and how I was reading it." Ten-Year-Old

"The best books I have ever read!" Eighty-Five-Year-Old

"I am in LOVE with the Challenge Series. My mom, sister and I have read them all together. Seriously some of the best books I have ever read." Sixteen-Year-Old

"I could smell the coffee and the baked goods and feel the beautiful cold snowy weather in Minnesota and the warmth of the old Victorian mansion. The criminal element was intriguing. The romance and interpersonal relationships were meaningful and sweet. The ability to describe the criminal element without any horrifying scenes was brilliant." Retail Customer

"I just finished the fifth Challenge Series novel last night. I saved each one for a relaxing treat before falling asleep. I loved them! The characters are believable, the story lines are engaging, and the adventures are quite exciting! I thoroughly enjoyed each book! Thank you so much for being such imaginative authors!" Goodreads Review

Received a long and very positive review from BookLife.

The Ambassadors

Real science plus extraterrestrials

Aliens arrive to help humanity rather than to kill and destroy.

But powerful humans have vested interests in maintaining the status quo. An exciting, amusing, and romantic story for teens through seniors.

Comments about *The Ambassadors*

"The science fiction element about genetics was fascinating. What an unusual story line of aliens coming to earth and their mission." Retail Reader

"There's an excellent balance between the seriousness of the message the aliens are trying to convey and the lighthearted humor of their attempts to understand human culture. It's unusual to find a book that's fun and easy to read, but also makes you think." Amazon Reader

" The characters were likeable, the plot unique, the philosophical, political and human nature observations astute without being heavy." Retail Reader

"Very thought provoking and interesting! I enjoyed this book very much!" Goodreads Comment

Missionary and the Witch

Authentic Transylvanian folklore and culture make this an engaging story especially appropriate for young adults.

Evil spirits are consistent with biblical portrayals in this good-versus-evil tale.

"I'm not a reader. But I bought this novel and read it all the first night. I could not put it down." Retail Customer

"Missionary and the Witch is an honest human story rooted in biblical stories. The characters come face-to-face with real evil and never cease to pour into their community and loved ones." Michael

"Missionary and the Witch is a battle of good versus evil with supernatural elements, well-developed lead characters, a bit of romance, and an intriguing Transylvania setting complete with werewolves and vampires." Writer

"I loved the amazing verbal descriptions of Romania from a visual and historical perspective. I felt like the book was powerful and gripping. I could not put it down." Missionary

"The attention to detail, the vibrant colors, the exciting scenery, all come together to form a truly enjoyable adventure." Spencer – teenager

Purchasing Novels by Kit and Drew Coons:

Print, Kindle, or audible novels can be obtained at Amazon by entering Kit and Drew Coons plus the novel title. Click on the image for a description.

The More Than Ordinary Lives website has direct links to Amazon for all of Kit and Drew's novels and also opportunities to order signed print books from the authors at discounted prices.

https://morethanordinarylives.com